The Complete Tempest

The Complete Tempest

An Annotated Edition

Of

The Shakespeare Play

Donald J. Richardson

authorHOUSE®

AuthorHouse™ LLC
1663 Liberty Drive
Bloomington, IN 47403
www.authorhouse.com
Phone: 1-800-839-8640

Published by AuthorHouse   02/05/2014

ISBN: 978-1-4918-5851-6 (sc)
ISBN: 978-1-4918-5849-3 (hc)
ISBN: 978-1-4918-5850-9 (e)

Library of Congress Control Number: 2014902091

Other Books by Donald J. Richardson

Dust in the Wind, 2001

Rails to Light, 2005

Song of Fools, 2006

Words of Truth, 2007

The Meditation of My Heart, 2008

The Days of Darkness, 2009

The Dying of the Light, 2010

Between the Darkness and the Light, 2011

The Days of Thy Youth, 2012

Those Who Sit in Darkness, 2013

Just a Song at Twilight, 2014

The Complete Hamlet, 2012

The Complete Macbeth, 2013

The Complete Romeo and Juliet, 2013

The Complete King Lear, 2013

The Complete Julius Caesar, 2013

The Complete Merchant of Venice, 2013

The Complete Midsummer Night's Dream, 2013

The Complete Much Ado About Nothing, 2013

The Complete Twelfth Night, 2014

The Complete Taming of the Shrew, 2014

Table of Contents

For lovers of Shakespeare everywhere

About the Book

In only two plays—*The Comedy of Errors* and *The Tempest*-
-does Shakespeare observe the unities of time, action, and place.
While these apparent constraints seem to restrict the playwright,
they also demonstrate an artistry that transcends the apparent
restrictions, especially in *The Tempest*. The added themes of justice
satisfied and of young love realized make for a satisfying blend of
artistry and stagecraft.

About the Author

Donald J. Richardson continues to define his life (and existence) by teaching English Composition at Phoenix College.

The Tempest

ACT I

SCENE I. On a ship at sea: a tempestuous noise of thunder and lightning heard.

Enter a Master and a Boatswain

MASTER

1 Boatswain!

BOATSWAIN

2 Here, master: what cheer?

MASTER

3 Good, speak to the mariners: fall to't, yarely,

> **Good**: "an acknowledgment of the boatswain's reply. The punctuation differentiates this from the *good* in line 15, which means 'good fellow.'"; **yarely**: "smartly, nimbly" (Riverside, 1,661)

4 or we run ourselves aground: bestir, bestir.

Exit

Enter Mariners

BOATSWAIN

5 Heigh, my hearts! cheerly, cheerly, my hearts!

Cheerly: "perhaps trisyllabic and equivalent to the modern 'cheerily'" (Orgel, 97)

6 yare, yare! Take in the topsail. Tend to the

Take . . . topsail: "to check the drift to leeward" (Kittredge, 1); **tend**: "attend" (Riverside, 1,661)

7 master's whistle. Blow, till thou burst thy wind,

Blow . . . enough: "He addresses the storm." (Riverside, 1,166); **burst thy wind**: "become wind-broken (like an overridden horse)" (Kittredge, 1)

8 if room enough!

If room enough: "as long as we have sea-room, i.e. space in which to maneuver without going aground" (Riverside, 1,661)

Enter ALONSO, SEBASTIAN, ANTONIO, FERDINAND, GONZALO, and others

Alonso: "a variant of Alphonso, which is the normal English form" (Orgel, 97)

ALONSO

9 Good boatswain, have care. Where's the master?

10 Play the men.

Play: "ply, urge on (?)" (Riverside, 1,661); "act like men" (Langbaum, 37)

BOATSWAIN

11 I pray now, keep below.

Keep: "stay"
(Bevington, 3)

ANTONIO

12 Where is the master, boatswain?

BOATSWAIN

13 Do you not hear him? You mar our labor: keep your

Mar: "spoil, by
interfering with
and interrupting"
(Kittredge, 2); **keep**:
"remain in" (Bevington,
3)

14 cabins: you do assist the storm.

GONZALO

15 Nay, good, be patient.

Good: "good fellow"
(Bevington, 3)

BOATSWAIN

16 When the sea is. Hence! What cares these roarers

Hence: "get away"
(Bevington, 3); **cares**:
"A singular verb with
a plural subject is
common in Elizabethan
English, especially
when the subject gives a
collective idea or when
the verb precedes."
(Kittredge, 2); **roarers**:
"(1) turbulent waves;
(2) rowdies" (Riverside,
1,661)

17 for the name of king? To cabin: silence! trouble us not.

Donald J. Richardson

GONZALO

18 Good, yet remember whom thou hast aboard.

BOATSWAIN

19 None that I more love than myself. You are a

20 councillor; if you can command these elements to   **Councillor**: "member
of the King's council"
(Riverside, 1,661)

21 silence, and work the peace of the present, we will   **The present**: "the present
occasion; but *present* may
be a mistake for *presence*,
i.e. the King's presence
or presence chamber"
(Riverside, 1,661); "restore
the present to peace
(since as a councilor his
job is to quell disorder)"
(Langbaum, 38)

22 not hand a rope more; use your authority: if you   **Hand**: "handle"
(Langbaum, 38)

23 cannot, give thanks you have lived so long, and make

24 yourself ready in your cabin for the mischance of   **Mischance**: "misfortune"
(Bevington, 4)

25 the hour, if it so hap. Cheerly, good hearts! Out   **Hap**: "happen"
(Bevington, 4)

26 of our way, I say.

Exit

GONZALO

27 I have great comfort from this fellow: methinks he   **Methinks ... gallows**:
"alluding to the proverb
'He that is born to be

4

hanged need fear no
drowning."'
(Riverside, 1,661)

28 hath no drowning mark upon him; his complexion is **Complexion**: "appearance
(as reflecting his
temperament)"
(Riverside, 1,661)

29 perfect gallows. Stand fast, good Fate, to his

30 hanging: make the rope of his destiny our cable, **Make . . . advantage**:
"make the rope that will
hang him our anchor
chain, since our actual one
now does us little good"
(Riverside, 1,661)

31 for our own doth little advantage. If he be not **Doth little advantage**:
"gives us little advantage"
(Langbaum, 38)

32 born to be hanged, our case is miserable. **Case is miserable**:
"circumstances are
desperate" (Bevington, 4)

Exeunt

Re-enter Boatswain

BOATSWAIN

33 Down with the topmast! yare! lower, lower! Bring **Bring . . . main-course**:
"keep her close to the
wind by means of the
mainsail"
(Riverside, 1,662)

34 her to try with main-course.

A cry within

5

35 A plague upon this howling! they are louder than

> **They are louder . . . office**: "these passengers make more noise than the tempest or than we do at our work" (Langbaum, 38)

36 the weather or our office.

> **Office**: "duties" (Riverside, 1,662); **our office**: "the noise we make while doing our jobs" (Kittredge, 2)

Re-enter SEBASTIAN, ANTONIO, and GONZALO

37 Yet again! what do you here? Shall we give o'er

> **Give o'er**: "give up" (Riverside, 1,662)

38 and drown? Have you a mind to sink?

SEBASTIAN

39 A pox o' your throat, you bawling, blasphemous,

40 incharitable dog!

> **Incharitable**: "ill-tempered" (Kittredge, 2)

BOATSWAIN

41 Work you then.

ANTONIO

42 Hang, cur! hang, you whoreson, insolent noisemaker!

> **Whoreson**: "bastard" (Kittredge, 2)

43 We are less afraid to be drowned than thou art.

GONZALO

44 I'll warrant him for drowning; though the ship were

> **Warrant him**: "guarantee him against" (Riverside, 1,662)

45 no stronger than a nutshell and as leaky as an

As an ... witch: "Both E.A.M. Colman (*Dramatic Use of Bawdy*) and Eric Partridge (*Shakespeare's Bawdy*) take the joke to be about menstruation without the use of absorbent padding, but *unstanched* can mean unsatisfied, and *leaky* may therefore instead imply sexual arousal." (Orgel, 99)

46 unstanched wench.

Unstanched wench: "loose woman, literally, one incapable of containing water" (Kittredge, 3)

BOATSWAIN

47 Lay her a-hold, a-hold! set her two courses off to

A-hold: "a-hull, close to the wind"; **set ... sea**: "i.e. set her mainsail and foresail so as to get her out to sea" (Riverside, 1,662)

48 sea again; lay her off.

Lay her off: "get her out to sea" (Orgel, 100)

Enter Mariners wet

MARINERS

49 All lost! to prayers, to prayers! all lost!

BOATSWAIN

50 What, must our mouths be cold?

Must our ... cold: "to be cold in the mouth, i.e. dead, was proverbial (Dent M1260.1). Some editors interpret the line to

mean that the
Boatswain here
swigs a drink,
thereby providing
some basis for
Antonio's charge of
drunkenness at l.
54" (Orgel, 100)

GONZALO

51 The king and prince at prayers! let's assist them,

52 For our case is as theirs.

SEBASTIAN

53 I'm out of patience.

ANTONIO

54 We are merely cheated of our lives by drunkards:

Merely: "utterly"
(Riverside, 1,662)

55 This wide-chopp'd rascal--would thou mightst lie drowning

Wide-chopp'd:
"wide-jawed,
wide-mouthed,
bawling—
and insolent"
(Kittredge, 3)

56 The washing of ten tides!

Ten tides: "Pirates
were hanged on
shore and left until
three tides had
washed over them."
(Riverside, 1,662)

GONZALO

57 He'll be hang'd yet,

58 Though every drop of water swear against it

59 And gape at wid'st to glut him.

Gape . . . him: "open its mouth to the widest to gulp him down" (Riverside, 1,662)

A confused noise within: "Mercy on us!"—"We split, we split!"—"Farewell, my wife and children!"—"Farewell, brother!"—"We split, we split, we split!"

ANTONIO

60 Let's all sink with the king.

SEBASTIAN

61 Let's take leave of him.

Exeunt ANTONIO and SEBASTIAN

GONZALO

62 Now would I give a thousand furlongs of sea for an

63 acre of barren ground, long heath, brown furze, any

Heath . . . furze: "heather . . . gorse (plants that grow in poor soil)" (Riverside, 1,662); **furze**: "prickly bushes of no value" (Kittredge, 4)

64 thing. The wills above be done! but I would fain

Fain: "gladly" (Riverside, 1,662)

65 die a dry death.

Exeunt

SCENE II. The island. Before PROSPERO'S cell.

Enter PROSPERO and MIRANDA

Prospero: "the name means 'fortunate' or 'prosperous' (literally

9

'according to one's
hopes')" (Orgel, 101)

MIRANDA

Miranda: "literally
'wonderful', 'to be
wondered at'" (Orgel, 101)

1 If by your art, my dearest father, you have

Art: "magic"
(Riverside, 1,662)

2 Put the wild waters in this roar, allay them.

Roar: "uproar"; **allay**:
"pacify" (Bevington, 6)

3 The sky, it seems, would pour down stinking pitch,

Pitch: "implying chiefly
its smell and blackness
here, but also with moral
overtones ('pitch defiles')
and possibly an ironic
ambiguity as well; its
practical use was for
caulking ships"
(Orgel, 101)

4 But that the sea, mounting to the welkin's cheek,

Welkin's: "sky's"; **cheek**:
"(1) face; (2) side of a
grate" (Riverside, 1,662)

5 Dashes the fire out. O, I have suffered

Fire: "the lightning,
imagined as boiling the
pitch of l. 3" (Orgel, 101)

6 With those that I saw suffer: a brave vessel,

Brave: "splendid"
(Riverside, 1,662); "fine,
gallant" (Langbaum, 40)

7 Who had, no doubt, some noble creature in her,

8 Dash'd all to pieces. O, the cry did knock

9 Against my very heart. Poor souls, they perish'd.

10 Had I been any god of power, I would

God of power: "The
power is both Prospero's
magic generally, and,

specifically, the raising of storms, as in George Herbert's 'The Bag' (c. 1630), ll. 5 and 9: 'Storms are the triumph of his art . . . The God of Power, as he did ride . . . '"
(Orgel, 101)

11 Have sunk the sea within the earth or ere

Or ere: "before" (Riverside, 1,662)

12 It should the good ship so have swallow'd and

13 The fraughting souls within her.

Fraughting: "forming the cargo" (Riverside, 1,662)

PROSPERO

14 Be collected:

Collected: "composed" (Riverside, 1,662)

15 No more amazement: tell your piteous heart

Amazement: "terror"; **piteous**: "pitying" (Riverside, 1,662)

16 There's no harm done.

MIRANDA

17 O, woe the day!

PROSPERO

18 No harm.

19 I have done nothing but in care of thee,

But: "except" (Bevington, 6)

20 Of thee, my dear one, thee, my daughter, who

21 Art ignorant of what thou art, nought knowing

22 Of whence I am, nor that I am more better

More better: "of higher rank (common Elizabethan double comparative)" (Riverside, 1,662)

23 Than Prospero, master of a full poor cell,

Full: "very" (Riverside, 1,662); **cell**: "technically a single-chamber dwelling, often with monastic implications; by the late-sixteenth century used poetically for 'a small and humble dwelling, a cottage' (OED); not applied to prisons until the eighteenth century" (Orgel, 102)

24 And thy no greater father.

No greater: "i.e. of no loftier position than is implied by his 'full poor cell'" (Riverside, 1,662)

MIRANDA

25 More to know

26 Did never meddle with my thoughts.

Meddle with: "mingle with, enter" (Riverside, 1,662); "the original meaning is 'mix with' with a sexual connotation persisting until well into the seventeenth century. The modern pejorative usage 'interfere with', appears to be the most common one by Shakespeare's time" (Orgel, 102)

PROSPERO

27 'Tis time

28 I should inform thee farther. Lend thy hand,

29 And pluck my magic garment from me. So:

Magi
Lie .
refer:
offic

Lays down his mantle

30 Lie there, my art. Wipe thou thine eyes; have comfort.

31 The direful spectacle of the wrack, which touch'd

Spectacle: "the predominant meaning is 'theatrical display or pageant', 'safely ordered' by Prospero as presenter, l. 34" (Orgel, 103) ; **wrack**: "shipwreck" (Riverside, 1,662); **touch'd . . . compassion**: "penetrated to the very soul of thy compassion; moved thy compassionate nature to its utmost depths" (Kittredge, 5)

32 The very virtue of compassion in thee,

Virtue: "essence" (Riverside, 1,662)

33 I have with such provision in mine art

Provision: "foresight" (Riverside, 1,662)

34 So safely ordered that there is no soul--

Ordered: "arranged" (Kittredge, 5); **soul--**: "The sentence changes its course in what follows, but the sense is plain." (Riverside, 1,662)

35 No, not so much perdition as an hair

Perdition: "loss" (Riverside, 1,662)

36 Betid to any creature in the vessel

Betid: "happened" (Riverside, 1,662)

ich thou heard'st cry, which thou saw'st sink. Sit down;

Which: "whom"
(Bevington, 7)

38 For thou must now know farther.

MIRANDA

39 You have often

40 Begun to tell me what I am, but stopp'd

41 And left me to a bootless inquisition,

Bootless inquisition: "useless inquiry"
(Riverside, 1,662)

42 Concluding "Stay: not yet."

PROSPERO

43 The hour's now come;

44 The very minute bids thee ope thine ear;

Ope: "open"
(Bevington, 7)

45 Obey and be attentive. Canst thou remember

Obey: "i.e. listen"
(Riverside, 1,662)

46 A time before we came unto this cell?

47 I do not think thou canst, for then thou wast not

48 Out three years old.

Out: "fully"
(Riverside, 1,662)

MIRANDA

49 Certainly, sir, I can.

PROSPERO

50 By what? by any other house or person?

By what: "i.e. by what image (in your memory)" (Orgel, 103)

51 Of any thing the image tell me that

Of . . . me: "describe to me whatever: the memory is assumed to be visual" (Orgel, 104)

52 Hath kept with thy remembrance.

MIRANDA

53 'Tis far off

54 And rather like a dream than an assurance

Assurance: "certainty" (Riverside, 1,663)

55 That my remembrance warrants. Had I not

Remembrance warrants: "memory guarantees" (Riverside, 1,663)

56 Four or five women once that tended me?

Tended: "attended" (Bevington, 7)

PROSPERO

57 Thou hadst, and more, Miranda. But how is it

58 That this lives in thy mind? What seest thou else

59 In the dark backward and abysm of time?

Backward . . . time: "abyss of the past" (Riverside, 1,663)

60 If thou remember'st aught ere thou camest here,

Aught: "anything" (Bevington, 8)

61 How thou camest here thou mayst.

MIRANDA

62 But that I do not.

PROSPERO

63 Twelve year since, Miranda, twelve year since,

Year: "often used as a plural" (Orgel, 104)

64 Thy father was the Duke of Milan and

65 A prince of power.

MIRANDA

66 Sir, are not you my father?

PROSPERO

67 Thy mother was a piece of virtue, and

Piece: "masterpiece"; **virtue**: "chastity" (Riverside, 1,663)

68 She said thou wast my daughter; and thy father

69 Was Duke of Milan; and thou his only heir

70 And princess no worse issued.

No worse issued: "no less noble in birth" (Riverside, 1,663)

MIRANDA

71 O the heavens!

72 What foul play had we, that we came from thence?

73 Or blessed was't we did?

PROSPERO

74 Both, both, my girl:

75 By foul play, as thou say'st, were we heaved thence,

76 But blessedly holp hither.

Blessedly holp: "providentially helped" (Riverside, 1,663)

MIRANDA

77 O, my heart bleeds

78 To think o' the teen that I have turn'd you to,

Teen: "sorrow, trouble"; **turn'd you to**: "reminded you of" (Riverside, 1,663)

79 Which is from my remembrance! Please you, farther.

From: "out of" (Riverside, 1,663)

PROSPERO

80 My brother and thy uncle, call'd Antonio--

81 I pray thee, mark me--that a brother should

82 Be so perfidious!--he whom next thyself

Next: "next to" (Bevington, 8)

83 Of all the world I loved and to him put

Put: "entrusted" (Kittredge, 6)

84 The manage of my state; as at that time

Manage: "administration" (Orgel, 105); **state**: "government" (Kittredge, 6)

85 Through all the signories it was the first

Signories: "city states" (Riverside, 1,663); **First**: "most prominent" (Kittredge, 6)

86 And Prospero the prime duke, being so reputed

Prime: "chief, first in rank" (Riverside, 1,663)

87 In dignity, and for the liberal arts

Liberal arts: "technically those 'considered worthy of a free man'" (Orgel, 105); "pursuits of learning and scholarship" (Kittredge, 6)

88 Without a parallel; those being all my study,

89 The government I cast upon my brother

90 And to my state grew stranger, being transported

To my . . . stranger: "withdrew from my position as ruler" (Kittredge, 7); **state**: "the dukedom—either the office or the country"; **transported / And rapt**: "both words literally mean 'physically carried away': Prospero describes his studies as a prefiguration of his abduction and dispatch to the island" (Orgel, 105)

91 And rapt in secret studies. Thy false uncle--

92 Dost thou attend me?

Dost thou attend me?: "are you listening?" (Kittredge, 7)

MIRANDA

93 Sir, most heedfully.

PROSPERO

94 Being once perfected how to grant suits,

Perfected: "expert in" (Riverside, 1,663)

95 How to deny them, who to advance and who

96 To trash for over-topping, new created

Trash for over-topping: "restrain from becoming too powerful. Two images are combined here: *trash* = check a hunting dog from going too fast; *overtopping* = growing too high." (Riverside, 1,663); **new created . . . mine**: "transformed my former followers" (Kittredge, 7)

97 The creatures that were mine, I say, or changed 'em,

Creatures: "dependents (whose office have been *created*)" (Orgel, 106); **or**: "either" (Riverside, 1,663)

98 Or else new form'd 'em; having both the key

Both . . . office: "control over both officials and administration" (Orgel, 106); **key**: "(1) key to office; (2) tuning key" (Riverside, 1,663)

99 Of officer and office, set all hearts i' the state

100 To what tune pleased his ear; that now he was

That: "so that" (Orgel, 106)

101 The ivy which had hid my princely trunk,

102 And suck'd my verdure out on't. Thou attend'st not.

Verdure: "vigor, vitality"; **on't**: "of it" (Riverside, 1,663)

MIRANDA

103 O, good sir, I do.

PROSPERO

104 I pray thee, mark me.

105 I, thus neglecting worldly ends, all dedicated

106 To closeness and the bettering of my mind

Closeness: "seclusion" (Riverside, 1,663)

107 With that which, but by being so retired,

With that . . . evil nature: "i.e., with that dedication to the mind which, were it not that it kept me from exercising the duties of my office would surpass in value all ordinary estimate, I awakened evil in my brother's nature" (Langbaum, 44); **but**: "merely" (Orgel, 106)

108 O'er-prized all popular rate, in my false brother

O'er-prized . . . rate: "had greater worth than any vulgar evaluation would place upon it" (Riverside, 1,663)

109 Awaked an evil nature; and my trust,

110 Like a good parent, did beget of him

Good parent: "That a good parent often bred a bad child was proverbial." (Riverside, 1,663); **of him**: "from him, on his part" (Kittredge, 8)

111 A falsehood in its contrary as great

A falsehood . . . as great: "a treachery as great in its contrariety to my trust" (Kittredge, 8)

112 As my trust was; which had indeed no limit,

No limit: "his treachery, then, was as boundless for treachery as my trust was for trust; he betrayed my trust in every possible point" (Kittredge, 8)

113 A confidence sans bound. He being thus lorded,

Sans: "without"; **lorded**: "i.e. established in a position of power" (Riverside, 1,663)

114 Not only with what my revenue yielded,

115 But what my power might else exact, like one

Else: "otherwise, additionally" (Bevington, 9); **like one . . . / Who having . . . of it**: "i.e., like one who really had these things—by repeatedly saying he had them (*into* = unto)" (Langbaum, 44)

116 Who having into truth, by telling of it,

Who . . . lie: "i.e., who, by repeatedly telling the lie (that he was indeed Duke of Milan), made his memory such a confirmed sinner against truth that he began to believe his own lie" (Bevington, 10); **into**: "unto, against (*into truth* modifies *sinner*)" (Riverside, 1,663)

117 Made such a sinner of his memory,

118 To credit his own lie, he did believe

To: "as to" (Riverside, 1,663)

119 He was indeed the duke; out o' the substitution

Out: "as a result" (Riverside, 1,663)

120 And executing the outward face of royalty,

Executing . . . royalty: "performing all of the functions of a ruler" (Kittredge, 9)

121 With all prerogative: hence his ambition growing--

122 Dost thou hear?

MIRANDA

123 Your tale, sir, would cure deafness.

PROSPERO

124 To have no screen between this part he play'd

No . . . for: "i.e. no separation between acting as Duke and being Duke" (Riverside, 1,663)

125 And him he play'd it for, he needs will be

Needs: "necessarily" (Bevington, 10)

126 Absolute Milan. Me, poor man, my library

Absolute Milan: "actual Duke of Milan" (Riverside, 1,663); **me**: "as for me" (Orgel, 107)

127 Was dukedom large enough: of temporal royalties

Temporal royalties: "practical administration" (Riverside, 1,663); **temporal**: "worldly, as opposed to spiritual" (Kittredge, 9)

128 He thinks me now incapable; confederates--

Confederates: "makes a corrupt bargain" (Kittredge, 9)

129 So dry he was for sway--wi' the King of Naples

Dry: "thirsty" (Riverside, 1,663); **sway**: "power" (Bevington, 10)

130 To give him annual tribute, do him homage,

Him: "i.e., the King of Naples" (Bevington, 10)

131 Subject his coronet to his crown and bend

His . . . his: "Antonio's . . . the King of Naples's" ; **bend**: "make bow down" (Bevington, 10)

132 The dukedom yet unbow'd--alas, poor Milan!--

Yet: "hitherto" (Orgel, 107)

133 To most ignoble stooping.

MIRANDA

134 O the heavens!

PROSPERO

135 Mark his condition and the event; then tell me

Condition: "compact"; **event**: "outcome" (Riverside, 1,663)

136 If this might be a brother.

MIRANDA

137 I should sin

I should sin . . . bad sons: "Miranda takes Prospero's attack on Antonio to imply an accusation of adultery against Prospero's mother." (Orgel, 107)

138 To think but nobly of my grandmother:

But: "other than" (Bevington, 10)

139 Good wombs have borne bad sons.

PROSPERO

140 Now the condition.

141 The King of Naples, being an enemy

142 To me inveterate, hearkens my brother's suit;

Hearkens: "listens to" (Bevington, 10)

143 Which was, that he, in lieu o' the premises

Lieu . . . premises: "return for the pledge" (Riverside, 1,663)

144 Of homage and I know not how much tribute,

145 Should presently extirpate me and mine

Presently extirpate: "immediately remove" (Riverside, 1,663)

146 Out of the dukedom and confer fair Milan

147 With all the honors on my brother: whereon,

Whereon: "in pursuance of which agreement" (Kittredge, 9)

148 A treacherous army levied, one midnight

149 Fated to the purpose did Antonio open

Fated: "appointed by fate" (Orgel, 108)

150 The gates of Milan, and, i' the dead of darkness,

151 The ministers for the purpose hurried thence

Ministers ... purpose: "agents employed to do this"; **thence:** "from there" (Bevington, 11)

152 Me and thy crying self.

MIRANDA

153 Alack, for pity!

154 I, not remembering how I cried out then,

155 Will cry it o'er again: it is a hint

Hint: "occasion (literally 'something one seizes on')" (Orgel, 108)

156 That wrings mine eyes to't.

Wrings: "(1) constrains; (2) extracts moisture from" (Riverside, 1,665); **to't:** "for the purpose (Abbott 186)" (Orgel, 108)

PROSPERO

157 Hear a little further

158 And then I'll bring thee to the present business

159 Which now's upon's; without the which this story

160 Were most impertinent.

Impertinent: "irrelevant"
(Riverside, 1,664);
"inappropriate"
(Langbaum, 46)

MIRANDA

161 Wherefore did they not

Wherefore: "why"
(Bevington, 11)

162 That hour destroy us?

PROSPERO

163 Well demanded, wench:

Demanded: "asked"
(Bevington, 11); **wench**:
"originally a young
woman or girl child; also
in Shakespeare's time, 'a
familiar or endearing form
of address; used chiefly
in addressing a daughter,
wife or sweetheart'(OED
Ic)" (Orgel, 108)

164 My tale provokes that question. Dear, they durst not,

165 So dear the love my people bore me, nor set

Set ... bloody: "i.e., make
obvious their murderous
intent" (Bevington, 11)

166 A mark so bloody on the business, but

A mark so bloody:
"Those who came in at the
death were marked with
the blood shed by the deer
(Kermode)" (Orgel, 109)

Donald J. Richardson

167 With colors fairer painted their foul ends.

With ... ends: "i.e., undertook to accomplish the same end by less violent means" (Riverside, 1,664); **fairer**: "apparently more attractive" (Bevington, 11)

168 In few, they hurried us aboard a bark,

In few: "in short" (Riverside, 1,664); **bark**: "in fact, Milan is not a port" (Orgel, 109); "ship" (Bevington, 11)

169 Bore us some leagues to sea; where they prepared

170 A rotten carcass of a butt, not rigg'd,

Carcass: "'the decaying skeleton of a vessel' (OED 5)" (Orgel 109); **butt**: "tub" (Riverside, 1,664); "probably from the Italian 'botto.'" (Kittredge, 10)

171 Nor tackle, sail, nor mast; the very rats

Nor tackle: "neither rigging (i.e., the pulleys and ropes designed for hoisting sails)" (Bevington, 11)

172 Instinctively had quit it: there they hoist us,

Instinctively: "according to the common belief that rats forsake a ship that is destined to be lost" (Kittredge, 10); **quit**: "abandoned" (Bevington, 11)

173 To cry to the sea that roar'd to us, to sigh

174 To the winds whose pity, sighing back again,

175 Did us but loving wrong.

Did ... wrong: "i.e. only added to our discomfort" (Riverside, 1,664)

26

MIRANDA

176 Alack, what trouble

177 Was I then to you!

PROSPERO

178 O, a cherubim

Cherubim: "It is in the sense of infant angel that Shakespeare uses the word here." (Asimov, 654)

179 Thou wast that did preserve me. Thou didst smile.

180 Infused with a fortitude from heaven,

Infused: "filled (as by divine influence)" (Kittredge, 11)

181 When I have deck'd the sea with drops full salt,

Deck'd: "(1) adorned; (2) covered" (Riverside, 1,664); "wept salt tears into the sea" (Langbaum, 46)

182 Under my burthen groan'd; which raised in me

Which: "i.e. Miranda's smile" (Riverside, 1,664)

183 An undergoing stomach, to bear up

Undergoing stomach: "courage to endure" (Riverside, 1,664); "spirit of endurance" (Langbaum, 46)

184 Against what should ensue.

MIRANDA

185 How came we ashore?

PROSPERO

186 By Providence divine.

187 Some food we had and some fresh water that

188 A noble Neapolitan, Gonzalo,

189 Out of his charity, being then appointed

190 Master of this design, did give us, with

191 Rich garments, linens, stuffs and necessaries,

Stuffs: "supplies" (Bevington, 12)

192 Which since have steaded much; so, of his gentleness,

Steaded: "been of use"; **gentleness**: "character proper to one of high birth and cultivation" (Riverside, 1,664)

193 Knowing I loved my books, he furnish'd me

194 From mine own library with volumes that

Volumes: "i.e. books of magic" (Riverside, 1,664)

195 I prize above my dukedom.

MIRANDA

196 Would I might

Would: "I wish" (Bevington, 12)

197 But ever see that man!

But ever: "i.e., someday" (Bevington, 12)

PROSPERO

198 Now I arise:

Now I arise: "both literally, as Prospero prepares to exercise his control over the shipwreck victims, and figurative, as he sees his fortunes turn (compare 'my zenith . . . ', l. 211)." (Orgel, 110)

Resumes his mantle

199 Sit still, and hear the last of our sea-sorrow.

Sit still: "remain seated" (Orgel, 110); **sea-sorrow**: "sorrowful adventure at sea" (Bevington, 12)

200 Here in this island we arrived; and here

201 Have I, thy schoolmaster, made thee more profit

More profit: "to become better educated" (Kittridge, 11)

202 Than other princes can that have more time

Princes: "The title 'prince' could be used to honor either sex." (Riverside, 1,664)

203 For vainer hours and tutors not so careful.

Vainer: "less serious, less usefully employed" (Kittredge, 11); **careful**: "both caring and taking trouble" (Orgel, 110)

MIRANDA

204 Heavens thank you for't! And now, I pray you, sir,

205 For still 'tis beating in my mind, your reason

Beating: "working violently" (Riverside, 1,664)

206 For raising this sea-storm?

PROSPERO

207 Know thus far forth.

208 By accident most strange, bountiful Fortune,

Fortune, . . . lady: "Fortuna was characteristically fickle" (Orgel, 111)

209 Now my dear lady, hath mine enemies

My dear lady: "i.e. favorable to me" (Riverside, 1,664); "i.e., formerly my foe, now my patroness" (Langbaum, 47)

210 Brought to this shore; and by my prescience

211 I find my zenith doth depend upon

Zenith: "technically the highest point of the celestial sphere, and also, here, the top of Fortune's wheel; hence the culmination of Prospero's good fortune" (Orgel, 111)

212 A most auspicious star, whose influence

Influence: "power (astrological term)" (Riverside, 1,664)

213 If now I court not but omit, my fortunes

Omit: "disregard, 'fail or forbear to use' (OED)" (Orgel, 111); "neglect" (Langbaum, 47)

214 Will ever after droop. Here cease more questions:

215 Thou art inclined to sleep; 'tis a good dullness,

Good dullness: "timely sleepiness" (Riverside, 1,664)

216 And give it way: I know thou canst not choose.

Give it way: "let it happen (i.e., don't fight it)" (Bevington, 13); **choose**: "help it (for the sleep is caused by magic)" (Kittredge, 12)

MIRANDA sleeps

217 Come away, servant, come. I am ready now.

Come away: "come here" (Riverside, 1,664)

218 Approach, my Ariel, come.

Ariel: "The word means 'lion of God' or possibly 'hearth of God' and is meant as a poetic synonym for Jerusalem." (Asimov, 655)

Enter ARIEL

ARIEL

219 All hail, great master! grave sir, hail! I come

220 To answer thy best pleasure; be't to fly,

Answer ... pleasure: "perform what most pleases you" (Kittredge, 12); **be't ... clouds**: "Ariel declares himself at home in the fluid and volatile elements; Prospero adds 'earth' at l. 300)" (Orgel, 111)

221 To swim, to dive into the fire, to ride

222 On the curl'd clouds, to thy strong bidding task

Task: "put to the test" (Kittredge, 12)

223 Ariel and all his quality.

Quality: "(1) skill; (2) cohorts, minor spirits under him" (Riverside, 1,664)

PROSPERO

224 Hast thou, spirit,

225 Perform'd to point the tempest that I bade thee?

To point: "in detail" (Riverside, 1,664)

ARIEL

226 To every article.

Article: "The metaphor is of a legal document." (Orgel, 112)

227 I boarded the king's ship; now on the beak,

Beak: "prow" (Riverside, 1,664)

228 Now in the waist, the deck, in every cabin,

In the waist: "amidships"; **deck**: "In early craft there was a deck only at the stern, so that sixteenth-century writers sometimes use *deck* as equivalent to *poop* (OED 2)." (Orgel, 112)

229 I flam'd amazement: sometime I'ld divide,

Flam'd amazement: "struck terror by appearing as the flamelike phenomenon called St. Elmo's fire or the corposant" (Riverside, 1,664); "There is no St. Elmo. The name is thought to be a corruption of 'St. Erasmus,' the patron saint of Mediterranean sailors. The glow was thought to be the visible sign of the saint guarding them during the storm." (Asimov, 656)

230 And burn in many places; on the topmast,

231 The yards and boresprit, would I flame distinctly,

Boresprit: "bowsprit"; **distinctly**: "in separate places" (Riverside, 1,664)

232 Then meet and join. Jove's lightnings, the precursors

233 O' the dreadful thunder-claps, more momentary

234 And sight-outrunning were not; the fire and cracks

Sight-outrunning: "swifter than sight" (Bevington, 13); **cracks**: "sounds of thunder" (Kittredge, 13)

235 Of sulphurous roaring the most mighty Neptune

Sulphurous: "Sulphur was popularly associated with thunder and lightning, from its use in explosives." (Orgel, 113); **Neptune**: "Roman god of the sea" (Bevington, 14)

236 Seem to besiege and make his bold waves tremble,

237 Yea, his dread trident shake.

PROSPERO

238 My brave spirit!

Brave: "splendid" (Riverside, 1,664)

239 Who was so firm, so constant, that this coil

Coil: "uproar" (Riverside, 1,664)

240 Would not infect his reason?

ARIEL

241 Not a soul

242 But felt a fever of the mad and play'd

Of the mad: "such as madmen have" (Riverside, 1,664)

243 Some tricks of desperation. All but mariners

Tricks of desperation: "acts of desperate lunatics" (Kittredge, 13)

244 Plunged in the foaming brine and quit the vessel,

245 Then all afire with me: the king's son, Ferdinand,

Then ... me: "Many editors repunctuate lines 244-45 so as to make the phrase modify *vessel* rather than *son*." (Riverside, 1,664)

246 With hair up-staring,--then like reeds, not hair,-- **Up-staring**: "standing on end" (Riverside, 1,665)

247 Was the first man that leap'd; cried, "Hell is empty

248 And all the devils are here."

PROSPERO

249 Why that's my spirit!

250 But was not this nigh shore?

ARIEL

251 Close by, my master.

PROSPERO

252 But are they, Ariel, safe?

ARIEL

253 Not a hair perish'd;

254 On their sustaining garments not a blemish, **Sustaining garments**: "garments that bore them up in the water" (Riverside, 1,665)

255 But fresher than before: and, as thou badst me, **Badst**: "ordered" (Bevington, 14)

256 In troops I have dispersed them 'bout the isle. **Troops**: "groups" (Bevington, 14)

257 The king's son have I landed by himself;

258 Whom I left cooling of the air with sighs **Cooling of**: "cooling" (Bevington, 14)

259 In an odd angle of the isle and sitting, **Angle**: "corner" (Orgel, 113)

260 His arms in this sad knot.

In . . . knot: "i.e., crossed thus (Ariel illustrates with a gesture). Crossed arms indicated melancholy." (Riverside, 1,665)

PROSPERO

261 Of the king's ship

262 The mariners say how thou hast disposed

263 And all the rest o' the fleet.

ARIEL

264 Safely in harbor

265 Is the king's ship; in the deep nook, where once

Nook: "inlet, small bay" (Riverside, 1,665)

266 Thou call'dst me up at midnight to fetch dew

Midnight . . . dew: "the appropriate time and a common substance for the performance of magic. Caliban credits Sycorax with the use of 'wicked dew' at l. 379.)" (Orgel, 113)

267 From the still-vex'd Bermoothes, there she's hid:

Still-vex'd Bermoothes: "always stormy Bermuda islands" (Riverside, 1,665)

268 The mariners all under hatches stow'd;

269 Who, with a charm join'd to their suffre'd labor,

With a charm: "by means of a magic spell"; **their suff'red labor**: "the labor they have endured" (Riverside, 1,665)

270 I have left asleep; and for the rest o' the fleet

271 Which I dispersed, they all have met again

272 And are upon the Mediterranean float,   **Float**: "flood, sea"
(Riverside, 1,665)

273 Bound sadly home for Naples,

274 Supposing that they saw the king's ship wreck'd

275 And his great person perish.

PROSPERO

276 Ariel, thy charge

277 Exactly is perform'd: but there's more work.

278 What is the time o' the day?

ARIEL

279 Past the mid season.   **Mid season**: "noon"
(Riverside, 1,665)

PROSPERO

280 At least two glasses. The time 'twixt six and now **Two glasses**: "i.e. two hours past noon. The reference here and at 5.i.253 is to hour glasses, not to the half-hour glasses used by mariners." (Orgel, 114)

281 Must by us both be spent most preciously.   **Preciously**: "as if every minute were precious" (Kittridge, 14)

ARIEL

282 Is there more toil? Since thou dost give me pains, **Pains**: "duties, chores" (Riverside, 1,665)

283 Let me remember thee what thou hast promised, **Remember**: "remind"
(Riverside, 1,665)

284 Which is not yet perform'd me.

PROSPERO

285 How now? moody? **Moody**: "the first
indication of Ariel's
characteristic
rebelliousness"
(Orgel, 114)

286 What is't thou canst demand?

ARIEL

287 My liberty.

PROSPERO

288 Before the time be out? no more!

ARIEL

289 I prithee,

290 Remember I have done thee worthy service;

291 Told thee no lies, made thee no mistakings, served

292 Without or grudge or grumblings: thou didst promise **Didst**: "did"
(Kittredge, 14)

293 To bate me a full year. **Bate**: "remit" (Riverside,
1,665); "reduce my term of
service" (Langbaum, 50)

PROSPERO

294 Dost thou forget

295 From what a torment I did free thee?

Donald J. Richardson

ARIEL

296 No.

PROSPERO

297 Thou dost, and think'st it much to tread the ooze   **Ooze**: "mud at sea-bottom" (Riverside, 1,665)

298 Of the salt deep,

299 To run upon the sharp wind of the north,

300 To do me business in the veins o' the earth   **Do me**: "do for me" (Bevington, 16); **veins**: "underground streams, which were thought to correspond to veins of the body" (Riverside, 1,665)

301 When it is bak'd with frost.   **Bak'd**: "hardened" (Riverside, 1,665); "caked" (Langbaum, 50)

ARIEL

302 I do not, sir.

PROSPERO

303 Thou liest, malignant thing! Hast thou forgot

304 The foul witch Sycorax, who with age and envy   **Sycorax**: "The name is an invention of Shakespeare's, though it may have arisen out of the combination of Greek words for 'pig' and 'crow.'" (Asimov, 658); **envy**: "malice" (Riverside, 1,665)

305 Was grown into a hoop? hast thou forgot her?

Grown into a hoop: "bent double" (Kittredge, 15)

ARIEL

306 No, sir.

PROSPERO

307 Thou hast. Where was she born? speak; tell me.

ARIEL

308 Sir, in Argier.

Argier: "Algiers" (Riverside, 1,665)

PROSPERO

309 O, was she so? I must

310 Once in a month recount what thou hast been,

311 Which thou forget'st. This damn'd witch Sycorax,

312 For mischiefs manifold and sorceries terrible

313 To enter human hearing, from Argier,

314 Thou know'st, was banish'd: for one thing she did

For one thing she did: "She was pregnant (see l. 317) and pregnancy required the commutation of a capital sentence." (Orgel, 116); **one thing**: "one good service" (Kittredge, 15)

315 They would not take her life. Is not this true?

ARIEL

316 Ay, sir.

39

PROSPERO

317 This blue-ey'd hag was hither brought with child

Blue-ey'd: "with dark circles around the eyes" (Riverside, 1,665); "generally explained as 'with blue eyelids', implying pregnancy." (Orgel, 116);" a sign of exhaustion or debility" (Kittredge, 16); **with child**: "pregnant" (Bevington, 16)

318 And here was left by the sailors. Thou, my slave,

319 As thou report'st thyself, wast then her servant;

320 And, for thou wast a spirit too delicate

For: "because" (Riverside, 1,665)

321 To act her earthy and abhorr'd commands,

Earthy: "and therefore antithetical to Ariel's volatile nature" (Orgel, 116)

322 Refusing her grand hests, she did confine thee,

Hests: "commands" (Riverside, 1,665)

323 By help of her more potent ministers

Her . . . ministers: "her agents, spirits more powerful than thou" (Langbaum, 51)

324 And in her most unmitigable rage,

325 Into a cloven pine; within which rift

326 Imprison'd thou didst painfully remain

327 A dozen years; within which space she died

Died: "Sycorax, then, died sometime before Prospero came to the island, and thus more than twelve years ago. Caliban is therefore at least twenty-four at the time of the play, and was at least thirteen when Prospero arrived with the three-year-old Miranda." (Orgel, 116)

328 And left thee there; where thou didst vent thy groans

Vent: "utter" (Kittredge, 16)

329 As fast as mill-wheels strike. Then was this island--

Mill-wheels: "i.e., the clappers on mill-wheels" (Riverside, 1,665); **strike**: "i.e. the water" (Kittredge, 17)

330 Save for the son that she did litter here,

Save: "except"; **litter**: "give birth to" (Bevington, 17)

331 A freckled whelp hag-born--not honor'd with

Whelp: "offspring. (Used of animals.)" (Bevington, 17); **hag-born**: "child of a witch" (Kittredge, 17)

332 A human shape.

ARIEL

333 Yes, Caliban her son.

Caliban: "The name has entered the language to mean any brutal and debased person." (Asimov, 659)

PROSPERO

334 Dull thing, I say so; he, that Caliban

> **Dull . . . so**: "Prospero's vexation continues: 'Don't parrot what I say!'" (Orgel, 116)

335 Whom now I keep in service. Thou best know'st

336 What torment I did find thee in; thy groans

337 Did make wolves howl and penetrate the breasts

> **Penetrate the breasts / Of**: "i.e. arouse sympathy in" (Orgel, 117)

338 Of ever angry bears: it was a torment

339 To lay upon the damn'd, which Sycorax

340 Could not again undo: it was mine art,

> **Could . . . out**: "Prospero thus demonstrates that his magic is more powerful than Sycorax's." (Orgel, 117)

341 When I arrived and heard thee, that made gape

> **Gape**: "open wide" (Riverside, 1,665)

342 The pine and let thee out.

ARIEL

343 I thank thee, master.

PROSPERO

344 If thou more murmur'st, I will rend an oak

345 And peg thee in his knotty entrails till

> **His**: "its" (Riverside, 1,665)

346 Thou hast howl'd away twelve winters.

ARIEL

347 Pardon, master;

348 I will be correspondent to command

Correspondent:
"obedient"
(Riverside, 1,666)

349 And do my spiriting gently.

Do . . . gently: "perform
my tasks as a spirit
ungrudgingly"
(Riverside, 1,666)

PROSPERO

350 Do so, and after two days

351 I will discharge thee.

ARIEL

352 That's my noble master!

353 What shall I do? say what; what shall I do?

PROSPERO

354 Go make thyself like a nymph o' the sea: be subject

Like a . . . sea: "The
disguise is, of course,
logically pointless if Ariel
is invisible to everyone
except Prospero. But he
is visible to the audience,
and the costume is the
appropriate one to adopt
in singing to Ferdinand on
the shore." (Orgel, 117)

355 To no sight but thine and mine, invisible

Invisible . . . else:
"(Ariel is invisible to
everyone in the play
except Prospero . . .)"
(Langbaum, 52)

356 To every eyeball else. Go take this shape

357 And hither come in't: go, hence with diligence!

Exit ARIEL

358 Awake, dear heart, awake! thou hast slept well; Awake!

MIRANDA

359 The strangeness of your story put

360 Heaviness in me.   **Heaviness**: "drowsiness"
(Riverside, 1,666)

PROSPERO

361 Shake it off. Come on;

362 We'll visit Caliban my slave, who never

363 Yields us kind answer.

MIRANDA

364 'Tis a villain, sir,

365 I do not love to look on.

PROSPERO

366 But, as 'tis,

367 We cannot miss him: he does make our fire,   **Miss**: "do without"
(Riverside, 1,666)

368 Fetch in our wood and serves in offices   **Offices**: "services, duties"
(Kittredge, 17)

369 That profit us. What, ho! slave! Caliban!

370 Thou earth, thou! speak.

Earth: "in contrast to Prospero's other servant, the spirit of air" (Orgel, 118)

CALIBAN

371 [Within] There's wood enough within.

Within: "i.e. within the discovery place at the back of the stage" (Orgel, 118)

PROSPERO

372 Come forth, I say! there's other business for thee:

373 Come, thou tortoise! when?

When: "a common expression of impatience" (Riverside, 1,666)

Re-enter ARIEL like a water-nymph

Like: "in the shape of" (Riverside, 1,666)

374 Fine apparition! My quaint Ariel,

Quaint: "The word includes the senses of ingenious and skillful, curious in appearance, and elegant." (Orgel, 118)

375 Hark in thine ear.

ARIEL

376 My lord it shall be done.

Exit

PROSPERO

377 Thou poisonous slave, got by the devil himself

Got ... dam: "alluding to stories of sexual liaisons between witches and the devil" (Orgel, 119); **got**:

"begotten, conceived"
(Kittredge, 18)

378 Upon thy wicked dam, come forth!

Wicked: "both harmful and foul" (Orgel, 119); **dam**: "mother. (Used of animals.)" (Bevington, 18)

Enter CALIBAN

CALIBAN

379 As wicked dew as e'er my mother brush'd

Wicked: "poisonous" (Kittredge, 18); **dew . . . feather**: "Dew was a common ingredient of magical potions, required by Prospero as well as Sycorax: see l. 266. The raven was especially associated with witchcraft, and its Greek and Latin name, *koral/ corax*, is clearly related to the unexplained name Sycorax." (Orgel, 119)

380 With raven's feather from unwholesome fen

Raven's feather: "Since the raven was the traditional bird of ill-omen, it is appropriate that the witch use its feather." (Kittrege, 18); **fen**: "marsh, bog" (Bevington, 18)

381 Drop on you both! a south-west blow on ye

South-west: "The south wind is the foggy wind in England, and infection was thought to reside in fog and mist" (Kittridge, 18)

382 And blister you all o'er!

PROSPERO

383 For this, be sure, to-night thou shalt have cramps,

384 Side-stitches that shall pen thy breath up; urchins

Urchins: "hedgehogs; here, goblins in the shape of hedgehogs" (Riverside, 1,666)

385 Shall, for that vast of night that they may work,

For ... work: "during that long and desolate period of darkness during which they are permitted to perform their mischief. It was thought that malignant spirits lost their power with the coming of day." (Riverside, 1,666)

386 All exercise on thee; thou shalt be pinch'd

Pinch'd ... honeycomb: "covered with pinches as thoroughly as the honeycomb has cells" (Orgel, 119)

387 As thick as honeycomb, each pinch more stinging

As thick as honeycomb: "i.e., all over, with as many pinches as a honeycomb has cells" (Bevington, 19)

388 Than bees that made 'em.

'Em: "i.e., cells of the honeycomb" (Riverside, 1,666)

CALIBAN

389 I must eat my dinner.

390 This island's mine, by Sycorax my mother,

"Caliban bases his claim to the island on inheritance. If he is, as Prospero asserts, illegitimate, the claim would be invalid." (Orgel, 119)

391 Which thou takest from me. When thou camest first,

392 Thou strok'st me and made much of me, wouldst give me **Strok'st**: "for 'strok'dst'" (Orgel, 119)

393 Water with berries in't, and teach me how

394 To name the bigger light, and how the less, **Bigger light . . . less**: "the sun and the moon" (Kittredge, 19)

395 That burn by day and night: and then I loved thee

396 And show'd thee all the qualities o' the isle, **Qualities**: "special properties and natural resources" (Kittridge, 19)

397 The fresh springs, brine-pits, barren place and fertile:

398 Cursed be I that did so! All the charms **Charms**: "spells" (Orgel, 120)

399 Of Sycorax, toads, beetles, bats, light on you! **Toads, beetles, bats**: "Evil spirits in the service of witches were thought to take the shape of these creatures" (Kittredge, 19)

400 For I am all the subjects that you have,

401 Which first was mine own king: and here you sty me **Sty me**: "pen me up like a pig" (Orgel, 120)

402 In this hard rock, whiles you do keep from me

403 The rest o' the island.

PROSPERO

404 Thou most lying slave,

405 Whom stripes may move, not kindness! I have used thee, **Stripes**: "lashes" (Riverside, 1,666)

406 Filth as thou art, with human care, and lodged thee **Human**: "humane" (Riverside, 1,666)

407 In mine own cell, till thou didst seek to violate

408 The honor of my child.

CALIBAN

409 O ho, O ho! would't had been done!

410 Thou didst prevent me; I had peopled else **Peopled else**: "otherwise populated" (Bevington, 19)

411 This isle with Calibans.

MIRANDA **Miranda**: "Some editors make Prospero the speaker." (Riverside, 1,666)

412 Abhorred slave, **Abhorred**: "detestable" (Kittredge, 19)

413 Which any print of goodness wilt not take, **Print**: "imprint. The metaphor alludes at once to coinage, wax seals, and typography." (Orgel, 120)

414 Being capable of all ill! I pitied thee,   **Capable of**: "susceptible (only) to" (Orgel, 120)

415 Took pains to make thee speak, taught thee each hour

416 One thing or other: when thou didst not, savage,

417 Know thine own meaning, but wouldst gabble like

418 A thing most brutish, I endow'd thy purposes   **Purposes**: "meanings, desires" (Bevington, 20)

419 With words that made them known. But thy vild race,   **Vild**: "vile"; **race**: "nature" (Riverside, 1,666); **race**: "natural disposition; species, nature" (Bevington, 20)

420 Though thou didst learn, had that in't which

421 good natures   **Good natures**: "people naturally good" (Kittredge, 19)

422 Could not abide to be with; therefore wast thou   **Abide**: "endure" (Kittredge, 19)

423 Deservedly confined into this rock,

424 Who hadst deserved more than a prison.

CALIBAN

425 You taught me language; and my profit on't

426 Is, I know how to curse. The red-plague rid you   **Red-plague**: "bubonic plague, called 'red' because of one of its symptoms" (Kittredge, 20) **rid**: "destroy" (Riverside, 1,666)

427 For learning me your language!

Learning: "teaching"
(Riverside, 1,666)

PROSPERO

428 Hag-seed, hence!

Hag-seed: "offspring
of a female demon"
(Bevington, 20)

429 Fetch us in fuel; and be quick, thou'rt best,

Thou'rt best: "you had
better" (Riverside, 1,666)

430 To answer other business. Shrug'st thou, malice?

Answer other business:
"perform other tasks"
(Orgel, 121); **answer**: "be
ready for" (Kittredge, 20);
malice: "evil creature"
(Kittridge, 20)

431 If thou neglect'st or dost unwillingly

432 What I command, I'll rack thee with old cramps,

Old: "plenty of (with an
additional suggestion,
'such as old people have')"
(Langbaum, 55)

433 Fill all thy bones with aches, make thee roar

Aches: "pronounced
aitches" (Riverside, 1,666)

434 That beasts shall tremble at thy din.

CALIBAN

435 No, pray thee.

Aside

436 I must obey: his art is of such power,

437 It would control my dam's god, Setebos,

Setebos: "the name is
found in accounts of
Magellan's voyages as that
of a 'great devil' of the
Patagonians." (Orgel, 121)

Donald J. Richardson

438 and make a vassal of him.

PROSPERO

439 So, slave; hence!

Exit CALIBAN

Re-enter ARIEL, invisible, playing and singing; FERDINAND following
ARIEL'S song.

Invisible: "Ariel is of course visible to the audience but he wears a costume which by convention makes him invisible to other persons on the stage, except Prospero." (Riverside, 1666); **playing**: "probably a lute; later Ariel plays a tabor and pipe." (Orgel, 121)

440 Come unto these yellow sands,

441 And then take hands:

442 Curtsied when you have and kiss'd

Curtsied . . . have: "when you have curtsied" (Bevington, 21); **kiss'd . . . whist**: "either 'kissed the wild waves into silence' or 'kissed each other' until the wild waves are silent'." (Orgel, 122)

443 The wild waves whist,

Whist: "being hushed" (Riverside, 1,667)

444 Foot it featly here and there;

Foot it featly: "dance nimbly" (Bevington, 21)

445 And, sweet sprites, the burthen bear.

Sprites: "spirits" (Bevington, 21); **the burthen bear**: "bear the burden, i.e. the bass undersong" (Riverside, 1,667); "refrain" (Kittredge, 21)

446 Hark, hark!

BURTHEN [dispersedly, within]:

Dispersedly: "from several directions" (Riverside, 1,667); "i.e. not in unison" (Orgel, 122)

447 Bow-wow.

448 The watch-dogs bark!

BURTHEN [within]

449 Bow-wow

450 Hark, hark! I hear

451 The strain of strutting chanticleer

452 *Cry [within]* Cock-a-diddle-dow.

FERDINAND

453 Where should this music be? i' the air or the earth?

454 It sounds no more: and sure, it waits upon

Waits: "attends" (Orgel, 122); "is controlled by" (Kittridge, 21)

455 Some god o' the island. Sitting on a bank,

Bank: "sandbank" (Bevington, 21)

456 Weeping again the king my father's wreck,

457 This music crept by me upon the waters,

458 Allaying both their fury and my passion

Passion: "literally, suffering" (Orgel, 122)

459 With its sweet air: thence I have follow'd it,

Thence: "i.e., from the bank on which he sat" (Bevington, 21)

460 Or it hath drawn me rather. But 'tis gone.

461 No, it begins again.

ARIEL sings

462 Full fadom five thy father lies;

Fadom: "fathom" (Riverside, 1,667); "originally the measure of a man's outstretched arms from fingertip to fingertip, reckoned as 6 feet. The drowned father is thus 30 feet deep." (Orgel, 123)

463 Of his bones are coral made;

464 Those are pearls that were his eyes:

465 Nothing of him that doth fade

Nothing . . . sea-change: "no part of his body is lost, for what is seemingly destroyed is merely changed into something more beautiful." (Kittredge, 21)

466 But doth suffer a sea-change

467 Into something rich and strange.

468 Sea-nymphs hourly ring his knell

Knell: "announcement of a death by the tolling of a bell" (Bevington, 21)

BURTHEN *[within]*

469 *Ding-dong*

470 Hark! now I hear them,--Ding-dong, bell.

FERDINAND

471 The ditty does remember my drown'd father.

> **Ditty**: "words of the song"; **remember**: "commemorate" (Riverside, 1,667)

472 This is no mortal business, nor no sound

> **Mortal**: "both human, and pertaining to death: Ferdinand's perception grows as he muses on the song." (Orgel, 123)

473 That the earth owes. I hear it now above me.

> **Owes**: "owns" (Riverside, 1,667)

PROSPERO

474 The fringed curtains of thine eye advance

> **Fringed curtains**: "eyelids" (Kittedge, 21); **advance**: "raise" (Riverside, 1,667)

475 And say what thou seest yond.

MIRANDA

476 What is't? a spirit?

477 Lord, how it looks about! Believe me, sir,

478 It carries a brave form. But 'tis a spirit.

> **Brave**: "excellent, splendid" (Riverside, 1,667)

PROSPERO

479 No, wench; it eats and sleeps and hath such senses

480 As we have, such. This gallant which thou seest

Gallant: "'A man of fashion and pleasure; a fine gentleman', especially 'a ladies' man (OED, B1,3), often, as here, with playful or semi-ironic overtones" (Orgel, 123)

481 Was in the wreck; and, but he's something stain'd

But: "except that"; **something stain'd**: "somewhat disfigured" (Riverside, 1,667)

482 With grief that's beauty's canker, thou mightst call him

Canker: "worm that eats blossoms" (Riverside, 1,667)

483 A goodly person: he hath lost his fellows

Goodly: "handsome" (Kittredge, 22)

484 And strays about to find 'em.

MIRANDA

485 I might call him

486 A thing divine, for nothing natural

Natural: "as opposed to the artificial creations of, e.g., Prospero's masque" (Orgel, 124)

487 I ever saw so noble.

PROSPERO

488 [Aside] It goes on, I see,

It: "i.e. the charm" (Riverside, 1,667); "Miranda's love for Ferdinand; it is part of Prospero's plan that they fall in love." (Kittredge, 22)

489 As my soul prompts it. Spirit, fine spirit! I'll free thee

490 Within two days for this.

FERDINAND

491 Most sure, the goddess

Goddess: "Miranda, whom he now sees." (Kittredge, 22)

492 On whom these airs attend! Vouchsafe my prayer

Airs: "i.e. the music he has heard" (Riverside, 1,667); **vouchsafe my prayer ... remain**: "may my prayer induce you to inform me whether you dwell" (Langbaum, 57)

493 May know if you remain upon this island;

May know: "that I may know" (Orgel, 124); **remain**: "dwell" (Bevington, 22)

494 And that you will some good instruction give

495 How I may bear me here: my prime request,

Bear me: "conduct myself" (Orgel, 124); **prime**: "first, most important" (Riverside, 1,667)

496 Which I do last pronounce, is, O you wonder!

Wonder: "The epithet puns on Miranda's name." (Orgel, 124)

497 If you be maid or no?

Maid or no: "a mortal maiden or a goddess" (Kittredge, 22)

MIRANDA

498 No wonder, sir;

499 But certainly a maid.

FERDINAND

500 My language! heavens!

501 I am the best of them that speak this speech,

Best: "first in rank" (Riverside, 1,667)

502 Were I but where 'tis spoken.

Where 'tis spoken: "in Naples" (Kittredge, 22)

PROSPERO

503 How? the best?

504 What wert thou, if the King of Naples heard thee?

FERDINAND

505 A single thing, as I am now, that wonders

Single: "solitary (because he thinks that he and the King are one and the same), but he probably has in mind also the senses 'deserted' and 'helpless'" (Riverside, 1,667)

506 To hear thee speak of Naples. He does hear me;

He . . . me: "i.e. because I am he" (Orgel, 125)

507 And that he does I weep: myself am Naples,

And . . . weep: "i.e., and I weep at this reminder that my father is seemingly dead, leaving me heir" (Bevington, 23); **Naples**: "King of Naples" (Riverside, 1,667)

508 Who with mine eyes, never since at ebb, beheld

At ebb: "dry (a part of the continued sea-imagery in the play)" (Riverside, 1,667); "continually weeping" (Orgel, 125)

509 The king my father wreck'd.

MIRANDA

510 Alack, for mercy!

FERDINAND

511 Yes, faith, and all his lords; the Duke of Milan

512 And his brave son being twain.

> **His brave son**: "not mentioned elsewhere in the play" (Riverside, 1,667); **twain**: "two (of these lords)" (Langbaum, 58)

PROSPERO

513 [Aside] The Duke of Milan

514 And his more braver daughter could control thee,

> **More braver**: "more splendid" (Bevington, 23); **control**: "refute" (Riverside, 1,667)

515 If now 'twere fit to do't. At the first sight

516 They have chang'd eyes. Delicate Ariel,

> **Chang'd eyes**: "exchanged loving looks" (Riverside, 1,667); "i.e., fallen in love" (Langbaum, 58); **Delicate**: "graceful, artful" (Orgel, 125)

517 I'll set thee free for this.

To FERDINAND

518 A word, good sir;

519 I fear you have done yourself some wrong: a word.

Done . . . wrong: "an ironically polite way of charging him with lying" (Riverside, 1,667)

MIRANDA

520 Why speaks my father so ungently? This

521 Is the third man that e'er I saw, the first

522 That e'er I sigh'd for: pity move my father

523 To be inclined my way!

Be inclined my way: "favor my inclinations" (Kittredge, 23)

FERDINAND

524 O, if a virgin,

525 And your affection not gone forth, I'll make you

526 The queen of Naples.

PROSPERO

527 Soft, sir! one word more.

528 [*Aside*] They are both in either's powers; but this swift business

Both in either's: "each in the other's" (Bevington, 23)

529 I must uneasy make, lest too light winning	**Uneasy**: "difficult"; **light . . . light**: "easy . . . lightly esteemed" (Riverside, 1,667)
530 Make the prize light.	**Light**: "slightly valued, with a quibble on 'wanton, unchaste'" (Kittredge, 23)

To FERDINAND

531 One word more; I charge thee

532 That thou attend me: thou dost here usurp	**Attend**: "follow, obey" (Bevington, 24)
533 The name thou ow'st not; and hast put thyself	**Ow'st**: "own'st" (Orgel, 126)

534 Upon this island as a spy, to win it

535 From me, the lord on't.	**On't**: "of it" (Riverside, 1,667)

FERDINAND

536 No, as I am a man.

MIRANDA

537 There's nothing ill can dwell in such a temple:	**Temple**: "'Any place regarded as occupied by the divine presence' (OED 3)" (Orgel, 126); **There's . . . temple**: "Renaissance neo-Platonism held that a beautiful body was the outward sign of a beautiful soul." (Kittredge, 24)
538 If the ill spirit have so fair a house,	**If the ill . . . with't**: "and, being stronger, expel it" (Orgel, 126)

539 Good things will strive to dwell with't. **Will strive . . . with't**: "will use every effort to inhabit the same house as the ill spirit and, being more powerful, will drive that spirit out" (Kittredge, 24)

PROSPERO

540 Follow me.

541 Speak not you for him; he's a traitor. Come;

542 I'll manacle thy neck and feet together:

543 Sea-water shalt thou drink; thy food shall be

544 The fresh-brook muscles, wither'd roots and husks **Fresh-brook mussels**: "Fresh-water mussels are inedible." (Orgel, 126)

545 Wherein the acorn cradled. Follow.

FERDINAND

546 No;

547 I will resist such entertainment till **Entertainment**: "treatment" (Riverside, 1,668)

548 Mine enemy has more power.

Draws, and is charmed from moving **Charmed**: "magically prevented" (Riverside, 1,668)

MIRANDA

549 O dear father,

550 Make not too rash a trial of him, for

Rash: "harsh"
(Bevington, 24)

551 He's gentle and not fearful.

Gentle: "of high birth";
fearful: "frightening,
dangerous, or, perhaps,
cowardly" (Bevington, 24)

PROSPERO

552 What? I say,

553 My foot my tutor? Put thy sword up, traitor;

Foot: "subordinate.
(Miranda, the foot,
presumes to instruct
Prospero, the head.)"
(Bevington, 24)

554 Who makest a show but darest not strike, thy conscience

555 Is so possess'd with guilt: come from thy ward,

Ward: "defensive posture
(in fencing)"
(Bevington, 24)

556 For I can here disarm thee with this stick

Stick: "staff"
(Riverside, 1,668)

557 And make thy weapon drop.

MIRANDA

558 Beseech you, father.

PROSPERO

559 Hence! hang not on my garments.

MIRANDA

560 Sir, have pity;

561 I'll be his surety.

Surety: "guarantee"
(Bevington, 24)

PROSPERO

562 Silence! one word more

563 Shall make me chide thee, if not hate thee. What!

564 An advocate for an imposter! hush!

565 Thou think'st there is no more such shapes as he,

566 Having seen but him and Caliban: foolish wench!

567 To the most of men this is a Caliban   **To**: "in comparison with" (Riverside, 1,668)

568 And they to him are angels.

MIRANDA

569 My affections   **Affections**: "inclinations" (Riverside, 1,669)

570 Are then most humble; I have no ambition

571 To see a goodlier man.   **Goodlier**: "more handsome" (Kittredge, 25)

PROSPERO

572 Come on; obey:

573 Thy nerves are in their infancy again   **Nerves**: "sinews" (Riverside, 1,668)

574 And have no vigor in them.

FERDINAND

575 So they are;

576 My spirits, as in a dream, are all bound up.   **Spirits**: "vital powers" (Riverside, 1,668)

577 My father's loss, the weakness which I feel,

578 The wreck of all my friends, nor this man's threats,

579 To whom I am subdued, are but light to me,   **But**: "merely, otherwise
than" (Orgel, 127);
light: "unimportant"
(Bevington, 25)

580 Might I but through my prison once a day

581 Behold this maid: all corners else o' the earth   **All corners**: "any parts"
(Orgel, 128)

582 Let liberty make use of; space enough

583 Have I in such a prison.

PROSPERO

584 [Aside] It works.

To FERDINAND

585 Come on.

586 Thou hast done well, fine Ariel!

To FERDINAND

587 Follow me.

To ARIEL

588 Hark what thou else shalt do me.   **Do me**: "do for me"
(Riverside, 1,668)

MIRANDA

589 Be of comfort;

590 My father's of a better nature, sir,

591 Than he appears by speech: this is unwonted   **Unwonted**: "unusual" (Kittredge, 25)

592 Which now came from him.

PROSPERO

593 Thou shalt be as free

594 As mountain winds: but then exactly do   **Then**: "i.e. if that is to be so" (Orgel, 128); "till then" (Langbaum, 61)

595 All points of my command.

ARIEL

596 To the syllable.

PROSPERO

597 Come, follow. Speak not for him.

Exeunt

ACT II

SCENE I. Another part of the island.

Enter ALONSO, SEBASTIAN, ANTONIO, GONZALO, ADRIAN, FRANCISCO, and others **GONZALO**

1 Beseech you, sir, be merry; you have cause,

2 So have we all, of joy; for our escape

3 Is much beyond our loss. Our hint of woe

Beyond: "more important than" (Orgel, 128); **hint**: "occasion" (Riverside, 1,668)

4 Is common; every day some sailor's wife,

5 The masters of some merchant and the merchant

Masters . . . the merchant: "chief officers of some merchant vessel, and the owner of it" (Riverside, 1,668)

6 Have just our theme of woe; but for the miracle,

Just: "exactly" (Bevington, 26)

7 I mean our preservation, few in millions

8 Can speak like us: then wisely, good sir, weigh

9 Our sorrow with our comfort.

With: "against" (Riverside, 1,668)

ALONSO

10 Prithee, peace.

67

SEBASTIAN

11 He receives comfort like cold porridge.

Porridge: "broth. There is an underlying pun on p*eace* (line 9) and *pease*, i.e. peas, a common ingredient of porridge." (Riverside, 1,668)

ANTONIO

12 The visitor will not give him o'er so.

Visitor: "minister who visits the sick and bereaved, i.e. would-be comforter" (Riverside, 1,668); **give him o'er**: "leave him alone" (Orgel, 129)

SEBASTIAN

13 Look he's winding up the watch of his wit. By

Watch . . . strike: "'From the beginning of the seventeenth century "watches" (from the context clearly pocket watches) are often spoken of as striking' (OED, s. watch iv. 21)" (Orgel, 129)

14 and by it will strike.

GONZALO

15 Sir,--

SEBASTIAN

16 One: tell.

Tell: "count" (Riverside, 1,668)

GONZALO

17 When every grief is entertain'd that's offer'd,

That's: "that which is" (Langbaum, 62)

18 Comes to th' entertainer--

Entertainer: "sufferer. Sebastian puns on the sense 'innkeeper.'" (Riverside, 1,668)

SEBASTIAN

19 A dollar.

Dollar: "a continental coin" (Riverside, 1,668); "i.e. in payment: Sebastian quibbles on *entertainer* = performer." (Orgel, 129)

GONZALO

20 Dolor comes to him, indeed: you

Dolor: "sorrow" (Riverside, 1,668)

21 have spoken truer than you purposed.

SEBASTIAN

22 You have taken it wiselier than I meant you should.

Wiselier: "i.e., understood my pun" (Langbaum, 62); "with more perception, cleverness" (Kittredge, 28)

GONZALO

23 Therefore, my lord,--

ANTONIO

24 Fie, what a spendthrift is he of his tongue!

Donald J. Richardson

ALONSO

25 I prithee, spare.

Spare: "spare your words" (Langbaum, 62)

GONZALO

26 Well, I have done: but yet,--

SEBASTIAN

27 He will be talking.

ANTONIO

28 Which, of he or Adrian, for a good

Which of . . . first: "will first" (Langbaum, 62)

29 wager, first begins to crow?

SEBASTIAN

30 The old cock.

Old cock: "i.e. Gonzalo" (Riverside, 1,668)

ANTONIO

31 The cock'rel.

Cock'rel: "i.e. Adrian" (Riverside, 1,668)

SEBASTIAN

32 Done. The wager?

ANTONIO

33 A laughter.

Laughter: "a laugh (perhaps with pun on the sense 'a sitting of eggs,' consistent with the poultry imagery)" (Riverside, 1,668); "the winner will

have the laugh on the
loser" (Langbaum, 62)

SEBASTIAN

34 A match!

A match: "a bargain;
agreed" (Bevington, 27)

ADRIAN

35 Though this island seem to be desert,--

Desert: "uninhabited"
(Riverside, 1,668)

SEBASTIAN

36 Ha, ha, ha! So, you're paid.

Ha, ha, ha: "Antonio
wins the bet, since Adrian
spoke first, The winner
was entitled to laugh.
Accordingly most editors
reverse the speech prefixes
for lines 35 and 36."
(Riverside, 1,668); **you're
paid**: "i.e., you've had your
laugh" (Bevington, 27)

ADRIAN

37 Uninhabitable and almost inaccessible,--

Inaccessible: "double
entendre" (Bevington, 27)

SEBASTIAN

38 Yet,--

ADRIAN

39 Yet,--

ANTONIO

40 He could not miss't.

Miss't: "(1) escape saying 'yet'; (2) avoid the island" (Riverside, 1,669)

ADRIAN

41 It must needs be of subtle, tender and delicate

Must needs be: "has to be" (Bevington, 27); **subtle**: "gentle" (Orgel, 130)

42 temperance.

Temperance: "'mildness of weather or climate' (OED 4)" (Orgel, 130)

ANTONIO

43 Temperance was a delicate wench.

Temperance: "climate. Antonio puns on the word as a girl's name." (Riverside, 1669); **delicate**: "given to pleasure" (Orgel, 130)

SEBASTIAN

44 Ay, and a subtle; as he most learnedly delivered.

Subtle: "Sebastian develops the theme of delicacy: *subtle* here implies craftiness and (sexual) expertise; and with *learnedly*, plays on the sense of acute or speculative." (Orgel, 130); **delivered**: "reported, declared" (Kittredge, 29)

ADRIAN

45 The air breathes upon us here most sweetly.

SEBASTIAN

46 As if it had lungs and rotten ones.

ANTONIO

47 Or as 'twere perfumed by a fen.

Fen: "low land covered wholly or partly with water unless artificially drained" (Merriam-Webster)

GONZALO

48 Here is everything advantageous to life.

ANTONIO

49 True; save means to live.

Save: "except" (Bevington, 28)

SEBASTIAN

50 Of that there's none, or little.

GONZALO

51 How lush and lusty the grass looks! how green!

Lush: "The relevant meaning current in Shakespeare's time is 'soft, tender'." (Orgel, 130); **lusty**: "healthy" (Bevington, 28)

ANTONIO

52 The ground indeed is tawny.

Tawny: "parched tan or yellow" (Riverside, 1669)

SEBASTIAN

53 With an eye of green in't.

Eye: "spot" (Riverside, 1,669)

ANTONIO

54 He misses not much.

He . . . much: "i.e. Gonzalo's is the 'eye of green'." (Orgel, 131)

SEBASTIAN

55 No; he doth but mistake the truth totally.

But: "merely" (Bevington, 28)

GONZALO

56 But the rariety of it is,--which is indeed almost

Rariety: "Perhaps this spelling indicates an unusual pronunciation of the word by Gonzalo, which Sebastian mimics." (Riverside, 1,669); "strangest thing about the whole affair" (Kittredge, 29)

57 beyond credit,--

Credit: "belief" (Kittredge, 29)

SEBASTIAN

58 As many vouch'd rarities are.

Vouch'd: "guaranteed true" (Riverside, 1,669); **rarities**: "exceptional quality, unique phenomena" (Orgel, 131)

GONZALO

59 That our garments, being, as they were, drenched in

60 the sea, hold notwithstanding their freshness and

61 glosses, being rather new-dyed than stained with

62 salt water.

ANTONIO

63 If but one of his pockets could speak, would it not

If . . . lies: "i.e., the inside of Gonzalo's pockets are stained" (Langbaum, 64)

64 say he lies?

SEBASTIAN

65 Ay, or very falsely pocket up his report

Pocket up: "conceal suppress. One who failed to challenge a lie or an insult was said to 'pocket up' the injury" (Riverside, 1,669)

GONZALO

66 Methinks our garments are now as fresh as when we

67 put them on first in Afric, at the marriage of

68 the king's fair daughter Claribel to the King of Tunis.

SEBASTIAN

69 'Twas a sweet marriage, and we prosper well in our return.

ADRIAN

70 Tunis was never graced before with such a paragon to

Graced: "honored, adorned" (Kittredge, 30); **to**: "for" (Riverside, 1,669)

71 their queen.

GONZALO

72 Not since widow Dido's time.

Widow Dido: "Antonio's vigorous reaction has been variously explained.

Dido was indeed a
widow, and Aeneas a
widower, when they met,
and perhaps Antonio
is laughing at what he
considers Gonzalo's
prudery in referring to
her as widow rather than
as Aeneas' mistress.
Widow could also be
used of a wife separated
from or deserted by her
husband, and Antonio
may be laughing at
Gonzalo for prudish
evasion of the fact that
the deserted Dido was
not Aeneas' wife."
(Riverside, 1,669)

ANTONIO

73 Widow! a pox o' that! How came that widow in?

74 widow Dido!

SEBASTIAN

75 What if he had said "widower Aeneas" too? Good Lord,

76 how you take it!   **Take**: "understand,
                                       respond to, interpret"
                                       (Bevington, 29)

ADRIAN

77 "Widow Dido" said you? you make me study of that: **Study of**: "meditate on
                                                       (OED 2)" (Orgel, 131)

78 she was of Carthage, not of Tunis.

GONZALO

79 This Tunis, sir, was Carthage.

This ... Carthage:
"Tunis and Carthage were separate cities, though not far apart"
(Riverside, 1,669)

ADRIAN

80 Carthage?

GONZALO

81 I assure you, Carthage.

SEBASTIAN

82 His word is more than the miraculous harp; he hath

Miraculous harp:
"the legendary harp of Amphion, which raised the walls of Thebes. Gonzalo's error has created a whole new city."
(Riverside, 1,669)

83 raised the wall and houses too.

ANTONIO

84 What impossible matter will he make easy next?

SEBASTIAN

85 I think he will carry this island home in his pocket

86 and give it his son for an apple.

ANTONIO

87 And, sowing the kernels of it in the sea, bring

Kernels: "seeds"
(Riverside, 1,669)

88 forth more islands.

GONZALO

89 Ay.

Ay: "Probably a reassertion of the identity of the two cities. Antonio responds with a sarcastic expression of approbation." (Riverside, 1,669)

ANTONIO

90 Why, in good time.

In good time: "ironic: 'at long last'." (Orgel, 132)

GONZALO

91 Sir, we were talking that our garments seem now

Talking: "saying" (Bevington, 29)

92 as fresh as when we were at Tunis at the marriage

93 of your daughter, who is now queen.

ANTONIO

94 And the rarest that e'er came there.

Rarest: "most remarkable, beautiful" (Bevington, 29)

SEBASTIAN

95 Bate, I beseech you, widow Dido.

Bate: "except" (Riverside, 1,669)

ANTONIO

96 O, widow Dido! ay, widow Dido.

GONZALO

97 Is not, sir, my doublet as fresh as the first day I

Doublet: "close-fitting jacket" (Bevington, 29)

98 wore it? I mean, in a sort.

In a sort: "comparatively" (Riverside, 1,669)

ANTONIO

99 That sort was well fished for.

Sort: "lot" (Orgel, 132)

GONZALO

100 When I wore it at your daughter's marriage?

ALONSO

101 You cram these words into mine ears against

You . . . sense: "the image is of someone being fed against his will; *stomach* = appetite." (Riverside, 1,669); **sense**: "means both intention and perception" (Orgel, 132)

102 The stomach of my sense. Would I had never

103 Married my daughter there! for, coming thence,

Married: "given in marriage" (Bevington, 30)

104 My son is lost and, in my rate, she too,

Rate: "opinion" (Riverside, 1,669)

105 Who is so far from Italy removed

106 I ne'er again shall see her. O thou mine heir

107 Of Naples and of Milan, what strange fish

108 Hath made his meal on thee?

Made his meal: "fed himself" (Bevington, 30)

Donald J. Richardson

FRANCISCO

109 Sir, he may live:

110 I saw him beat the surges under him,

       Surges: "waves" (Kittredge, 31)

111 And ride upon their backs; he trod the water,

112 Whose enmity he flung aside, and breasted

113 The surge most swoln that met him; his bold head

114 Bove the contentious waves he kept, and oar'd

115 Himself with his good arms in lusty stroke

       Lusty: "vigorous" (Bevington, 30)

116 To the shore, that o'er his wave-worn basis bow'd,

       His wave-worn basis: "its foundation hollowed by the action of the sea" (Riverside, 1,669); **wave-worn basis bow'd**: "(the image is of a guardian cliff on the shore)" (Langbaum, 66)

117 As stooping to relieve him: I not doubt

       As: "as if"; **I not**: "I do not" (Bevington, 30)

118 He came alive to land.

       Came . . . land: "reached land alive" (Bevington, 30)

ALONSO

119 No, no, he's gone.

SEBASTIAN

120 Sir, you may thank yourself for this great loss,

121 That would not bless our Europe with your daughter,   **That**: "you who"
(Riverside, 1,669)

122 But rather loose her to an African;   **Rather**: "would rather"
(Bevington, 30); **loose**:
"with second (perhaps
primary) sense 'lose,'
often spelled *loose*"
(Riverside, 1,669)

123 Where she at least is banish'd from your eye,   **Is banished . . . eye**: "is
not constantly before
your eye to serve as a
reproachful reminder
of what you have done"
(Bevington, 30)

124 Who hath cause to wet the grief on't.   **Wet the grief on't**:
"weep over the sorrow of
it" (Orgel, 133)

ALONSO

125 Prithee, peace.

SEBASTIAN

126 You were kneel'd to and importuned otherwise   **Importuned**: "accented
on the second syllable"
(Orgel, 133); "urged,
implored" (Bevington,
30)

127 By all of us, and the fair soul herself

128 Weigh'd between loathness and obedience, at   **Weigh'd . . . bow**:
"weighed in the scale
her unwillingness to
marry and her duty of
obedience to her father,
to see which would
prevail"
(Riverside, 1,669)

129 Which end o' the beam should bow. We have lost

130 your son,

131 I fear, for ever: Milan and Naples have

132 Moe widows in them of this business' making   **Moe**: "more" (Riverside, 1,670); **of . . . making**: "on account of this marriage" (Bevington, 31)

133 Than we bring men to comfort them:

134 The fault's your own.

ALONSO

135 So is the dear'st o' the loss.   **Dear'st**: "heaviest, most costly" (Bevington, 31)

GONZALO

136 My lord Sebastian,

137 The truth you speak doth lack some gentleness

138 And time to speak it in: you rub the sore,   **Time**: "appropriate occasion" (Riverside, 1,670)

139 When you should bring the plaster.   **Plaster**: "'a healing or soothing means or measure' (OED i.1b)" (Orgel, 134)

SEBASTIAN

140 Very well.

ANTONIO

141 And most chirurgeonly.

Chirurgeonly: "like a
surgeon"
(Riverside, 1,670)

GONZALO

142 It is foul weather in us all, good sir,

143 When you are cloudy.

SEBASTIAN

144 Fowl weather?

Fowl: "Sebastian's pun
returns to the imagery
of ll. 28-31." (Riverside,
1,670)

ANTONIO

145 Very foul.

GONZALO

146 Had I plantation of this isle, my lord,--

Plantation: "colonization,
but the following speakers
take up the word in
the sense 'planting.'"
(Riverside, 1,670)

ANTONIO

147 He'ld sow't with nettle-seed.

SEBASTIAN

148 Or docks, or mallows.

Docks: "'coarse
weedy herbs' (OED
I), characterized as
'hateful' . . . because
they are . . . inimical to
productive cultivations. But

dock is also well-known as the popular antidote for nettle-stings' (OED Ia), hence presumably the association of the two as complementary weeds.";
mallows: "another weed, but also another antidote for Gonzalo's nettles" (Orgel, 135)

GONZALO

149 And were the king on't, what would I do?

SEBASTIAN

150 'Scape being drunk for want of wine.

'Scape: "escape"; **want**: "lack. (Sebastian jokes sarcastically that this hypothetical ruler would be saved from dissipation only by the barrenness of the island.)" (Bevington, 31)

GONZALO

151 I' the commonwealth I would by contraries

Contraries: "the opposite of what is customary" (Riverside, 1,670)

152 Execute all things; for no kind of traffic

Traffic: "business, trade" (Riverside, 1,670)

153 Would I admit; no name of magistrate;

154 Letters should not be known; riches, poverty,

Letters: "learning, literacy" (Riverside, 1,670)

155 And use of service, none; contract, succession,

Service: "servanthood, serving of some by others"; **succession**: "inheritance, hereditary

privilege"
(Riverside, 1,670)

156 Bourn, bound of land, tilth, vineyard, none;

Bourn: "boundary, i.e. division of land among individual owners"; **tilth**: "tillage" (Riverside, 1,670); "agriculture" (Langbaum, 67); **bound of land**: "landmarks" (Bevington, 32)

157 No use of metal, corn, or wine, or oil;

Corn: "grain" (Riverside, 1,670)

158 No occupation; all men idle, all;

Idle . . . pure: "countering the proverb 'Idleness begets lust' (Tilley 19)" (Orgel, 135); **occupation**: "working at a trade" (Kittredge, 33)

159 And women too, but innocent and pure;

160 No sovereignty;--

SEBASTIAN

161 Yet he would be king on't.

ANTONIO

162 The latter end of his commonwealth forgets the

163 beginning.

GONZALO

164 All things in common nature should produce

In common: "for communal use" (Orgel, 135)

165 Without sweat or endeavor: treason, felony,

166 Sword, pike, knife, gun, or need of any engine,   **Pike**: "spear"; **engine**: "instrument of war" (Riverside, 1,670); "weapon" (Langbaum, 67)

167 Would I not have; but nature should bring forth,

168 Of it own kind, all foison, all abundance,   **It**: "its"; **foison**: "plenty" (Riverside, 1,670)

169 To feed my innocent people.

SEBASTIAN

170 No marrying 'mong his subjects?   **No marrying**: "presumably not: marriage is a 'contract' (l. 155), and irrelevant to 'innocent people' (l. 169)" (Orgel, 136)

ANTONIO

171 None, man; all idle: whores and knaves.

GONZALO

172 I would with such perfection govern, sir,

173 To excel the golden age.   **The Golden Age**: "the age, according to Hesiod, when Cronos, or Saturn, ruled the world; an age of innocence and abundance" (Bevington, 32)

SEBASTIAN

174 'Save his majesty!   **'Save**: "God save" (Riverside, 1,670)

ANTONIO

175 Long live Gonzalo!

GONZALO

176 And,--do you mark me, sir?

ALONSO

177 Prithee, no more: thou dost talk nothing to me.

GONZALO

178 I do well believe your highness; and

179 did it to minister occasion to these gentlemen,

Minister occasion: "provide an opportunity (to laugh)" (Orgel, 136)

180 who are of such sensible and nimble lungs that

Sensible and nimble: "sensitive and lively" (Riverside, 1,670)

181 they always use to laugh at nothing.

Use: "are accustomed" (Orgel, 136)

ANTONIO

182 'Twas you we laughed at.

GONZALO

183 Who in this kind of merry fooling am nothing

184 to you: so you may continue and laugh at

185 nothing still.

ANTONIO

186 What a blow was there given!

Donald J. Richardson

SEBASTIAN

187 And it had not fallen flat-long.

And: "if"; **flat-long**: "with the sword blade flat, no on edge" (Riverside, 1,670)

GONZALO

188 You are gentlemen of brave mettle; you would lift

Brave mettle: "fine spirit" (Kittridge, 35); **mettle**: "the same word as *metal* . . . continuing Sebastian's sword metaphor"; **you would . . . changing**: "(1) You would try to steal the moon if it held still long enough; (b) the moon would have to stop changing before you would do anything extraordinary." (Orgel, 136)

189 the moon out of her sphere, if she would continue

Sphere: "orbit. (Literally, one of the concentric zones occupied by planets in the Ptolemaic astronomy.)" (Bevington, 33)

190 in it five weeks without changing.

Enter ARIEL, invisible, playing solemn music

SEBASTIAN

191 We would so, and then go a-bat-fowling.

A-bat-fowling: "(a) 'the catching of birds by night when at roost' (OED), here using the moon as a lantern; (b) 'swindling, victimizing the simple' (OED 2)" (Orgel, 137); "i.e., in order to gull

simpletons like you(?)"
(Langbaum, 68)

ANTONIO

192 Nay, good my lord, be not angry.

GONZALO

193 No, I warrant you; I will not adventure

Adventure ... weakly: "risk my reputation for good sense by getting angry at such superficial fellows" (Riverside, 1,670)

194 my discretion so weakly. Will you laugh

Discretion: "reputation for good sense" (Kittredge, 35)

195 me asleep, for I am very heavy?

Heavy: "drowsy" (Riverside, 1,670)

ANTONIO

196 Go sleep, and hear us.

Go ... us: "let our laughing send you to sleep, or, go to sleep and hear us laugh at you" (Bevington, 33)

All sleep except ALONSO, SEBASTIAN, and ANTONIO

ALONSO

197 What, all so soon asleep! I wish mine eyes

198 Would, with themselves, shut up my thoughts: I find

Would ... thoughts: "would shut off my melancholy brooding when they close themselves in sleep" (Bevington, 33)

199 They are inclined to do so.

SEBASTIAN

200 Please you, sir,

201 Do not omit the heavy offer of it:

Omit ... offer: "neglect the opportunity sleepiness provides" (Riverside, 1,670); **heavy**: "here including the sense 'serious'" (Orgel, 137)

202 It seldom visits sorrow; when it doth,

Visits: "see note to II.i.12" (Riverside, 1,670)

203 It is a comforter.

ANTONIO

204 We two, my lord,

205 Will guard your person while you take your rest,

206 And watch your safety.

ALONSO

207 Thank you. Wondrous heavy.

ALONSO sleeps. Exit ARIEL

SEBASTIAN

208 What a strange drowsiness possesses them!

ANTONIO

209 It is the quality o' the climate.

Quality: "nature, peculiarity" (Kittredge, 35)

SEBASTIAN

210 Why

211 Doth it not then our eyelids sink? I find not

Sink: "cause to close"
(Kittredge, 35)

212 Myself disposed to sleep.

ANTONIO

213 Nor I; my spirits are nimble.

Nimble: "on the alert"
(Kittredge, 35)

214 They fell together all, as by consent;

Consent: "common
agreement, consensus"
(Orgel, 137)

215 They dropp'd, as by a thunder-stroke. What might,

216 Worthy Sebastian? O, what might?--No more:--

217 And yet me thinks I see it in thy face,

218 What thou shouldst be: the occasion speaks thee, and

Speaks thee: "calls
upon you (to seize the
opportunity)"
(Riverside, 1,670)

219 My strong imagination sees a crown

220 Dropping upon thy head.

SEBASTIAN

221 What, art thou waking?

Waking: "awake"
(Orgel, 138)

ANTONIO

222 Do you not hear me speak?

SEBASTIAN

223 I do; and surely

224 It is a sleepy language and thou speak'st

225 Out of thy sleep. What is it thou didst say?

226 This is a strange repose, to be asleep

227 With eyes wide open; standing, speaking, moving,

228 And yet so fast asleep.

ANTONIO

229 Noble Sebastian,

230 Thou let'st thy fortune sleep--die, rather; wink'st   **Wink'st**: "keep your
eyes shut"
(Riverside, 1,671)

231 Whiles thou art waking.

SEBASTIAN

232 Thou dost snore distinctly;   **Distinctly**: "articulately,
'so as to be clearly
perceived or understood'
(OED 2)" (Orgel, 138)

233 There's meaning in thy snores.

ANTONIO

234 I am more serious than my custom: you

235 Must be so too, if heed me; which to do   **If heed**: "if you heed"
(Langbaum, 70)

236 Trebles thee o'er.   **Trebles thee o'er**:
"triples your fortune"
(Riverside, 1,671)

SEBASTIAN

237 Well, I am standing water.   **Standing water**: "i.e.
indecisive, going neither

forward nor back"
(Riverside, 1,671)

ANTONIO

238 I'll teach you how to flow.

Flow: "rise (as the tide)"
(Kittredge, 36)

SEBASTIAN

239 Do so: to ebb

To ebb . . . me: "(a) My
natural laziness prompts
me to withdraw; (b) The
idleness imposed on me by
my birth . . . teaches me to
hold back." (Orgel, 138-39)

240 Hereditary sloth instructs me.

Hereditary sloth:
"natural laziness and
the position of younger
brother, one who cannot
inherit" (Bevington, 34)

ANTONIO

241 O!

242 If you but knew how you the purpose cherish

Cherish: "enrich"
(Riverside, 1,671)

243 Whiles thus you mock it! how, in stripping it,

In stripping . . . invest it:
"In stripping the purpose
off you, you clothe
yourself with it all the
more" (Langbaum, 70)

244 You more invest it! Ebbing men, indeed,

Invest: "dress up"
(Riverside, 1,671)

245 Most often do so near the bottom run

The bottom: "i.e., on
which unadventurous
men go aground and
miss the tide of fortune"
(Bevington, 35)

246 By their own fear or sloth.

SEBASTIAN

247 Prithee, say on:

248 The setting of thine eye and cheek proclaim

Setting: "fixed look" (Riverside, 1,671)

249 A matter from thee, and a birth indeed

A matter: "something important" (Orgel, 139)

250 Which throes thee much to yield.

Throes: "causes labor pains" (Riverside, 1,671); **yield**: "give forth, speak about" (Bevington, 35)

ANTONIO

251 Thus, sir:

252 Although this lord of weak remembrance, this,

This lord: "i.e. Gonzalo"; **of weak remembrance**: "having a short memory (perhaps alluding to Gonzalo's lapse in identifying Tunis with Carthage); with following shift to the sense 'remembered only briefly after death.'" (Riverside, 1,671)

253 Who shall be of as little memory

Of as little memory: "as little remembered" (Langbaum, 71)

254 When he is earth'd, hath here almost persuade,--

Earth'd: "buried" (Riverside, 1,671)

255 For he's a spirit of persuasion, only

Only . . . persuade: "has no function except to persuade. Gonzalo is a privy councilor." (Riverside, 1,671)

256 Professes to persuade,--the king his son's alive,

257 'Tis as impossible that he's undrown'd

258 As he that sleeps here swims.

SEBASTIAN

259 I have no hope

260 That he's undrown'd.

ANTONIO

261 O, out of that "no hope"

262 What great hope have you! no hope that way is

> **That way**: "i.e., in regard to Ferdinand's being saved" (Bevington, 35)

263 Another way so high a hope that even

264 Ambition cannot pierce a wink beyond,

> **Wink**: "glimpse" (Riverside, 1,671)

265 But doubt discovery there. Will you grant with me

> **Doubt discovery there**: "is uncertain of seeing clearly even there" (Riverside, 1,671)

266 That Ferdinand is drown'd?

SEBASTIAN

267 He's gone.

ANTONIO

268 Then, tell me,

269 Who's the next heir of Naples?

Donald J. Richardson

SEBASTIAN

270 Claribel.

ANTONIO

271 She that is queen of Tunis; she that dwells

272 Ten leagues beyond man's life; she that from Naples

Ten . . . life: "thirty miles farther than a lifetime's journey" (Riverside, 1,671)

273 Can have no note, unless the sun were post--

Note: "news"; **post**: "messenger" (Riverside, 1,671)

274 The man i' the moon's too slow--till new-born chins

Moon's too slow: "The point is that the moon requires a month to complete its cycle, whereas the sun takes only a day." (Orgel, 140); **till new-born . . . razorable**: "till babies just born be ready to shave" (Langbaum, 71)

275 Be rough and razorable; she that--from whom?

Razorable: "ready for shaving" (Bevington, 36); **she that . . . seaswallow'd**: "she who is separated from Naples by so dangerous a sea that we were ourselves swallowed up by it" (Langbaum, 71); **from**: "coming from" (Riverside, 1,671)

96

276 We all were sea-swallow'd, though some cast again,   **Cast**: "(1) cast up;
(2) cast as actors"
(Riverside, 1,671)

277 And by that destiny to perform an act

278 Whereof what's past is prologue, what to come

279 In yours and my discharge.   **Discharge**:
"performance"
(Riverside, 1,671)

SEBASTIAN

280 What stuff is this! how say you?

281 'Tis true, my brother's daughter's queen of Tunis;

282 So is she heir of Naples; 'twixt which regions

283 There is some space.

ANTONIO

284 A space whose every cubit   **Cubit**: "measure
of about 20 inches"
(Riverside, 1,671)

285 Seems to cry out, "How shall that Claribel

286 Measure us back to Naples? Keep in Tunis,   **Measure us**: "i.e.
travel over the
cubits" (Riverside,
1,671); **keep**: "stay"
(Orgel, 141)

287 And let Sebastian wake." Say, this were death   **Wake**: "i.e.
awake to fortune"
(Riverside, 1,671)

288 That now hath seized them; why, they were no worse

289 Than now they are. There be that can rule Naples | **There be**: "there are those" (Bevington, 36)

290 As well as he that sleeps; lords that can prate | **Prate**: "speak foolishly" (Bevington, 36)

291 As amply and unnecessarily

292 As this Gonzalo; I myself could make | **Make . . . chat**: "train a jackdaw to speak as wisely as he. Jackdaws were taught to speak." (Riverside, 1,671)

293 A chough of as deep chat. O, that you bore | **chough**: "a bird of the crow family . . . (OED). For the figurative use, a chatterer or prater. . . . The word is also a variant spelling of *chuff*, a boor or churl, which provides a relevant ambiguity here." (Orgel, 141); **bore**: "had" (Kittredge, 39)

294 The mind that I do! what a sleep were this

295 For your advancement! Do you understand me?

SEBASTIAN

296 Methinks I do.

ANTONIO

297 And how does your content | **Content**: "inclination" (Riverside, 1,671)

298 Tender your own good fortune? | **Tender**: "regard" (Riverside, 1,671)

SEBASTIAN

299 I remember

300 You did supplant your brother Prospero.

ANTONIO

301 True:

302 And look how well my garments sit upon me;

303 Much feater than before: my brother's servants   **Feater:** "more gratefully" (Riverside, 1,671)

304 Were then my fellows; now they are my men.

SEBASTIAN

305 But, for your conscience?

ANTONIO

306 Ay, sir; where lies that? if 'twere a kibe,   **Kibe:** "chilblain" (Riverside, 1,671)

307 'Twould put me to my slipper: but I feel not   **Put me to:** "make me wear" (Riverside, 1,671)

308 This deity in my bosom: twenty consciences,

309 That stand 'twixt me and Milan, candied be they   **Milan:** "the dukedom of Milan"; **candied:** "sugared" (Riverside, 1,671); "The sense is probably 'congealed, frozen solid', rather than 'turned to sugar, glazed'." (Orgel, 142); **be they:** "may they be" (Bevington, 37)

310 And melt ere they molest! Here lies your brother,   **Melt:** "possibly an apocope for 'melted'" ;

99

molest: "interfere with me" (Orgel, 142)

311 No better than the earth he lies upon,

312 If he were that which now he's like, that's dead;

That's dead: "that is, if he were dead" (Langbaum, 73)

313 Whom I, with this obedient steel, three inches of it,

314 Can lay to bed for ever; whiles you, doing thus,

Doing thus: "Antonio mimes stabbing Gonzalo." (Orgel, 142)

315 To the perpetual wink for aye might put

To . . . put: "might put to sleep forever" (Orgel, 142); **wink**: "sleep" (Riverside, 1,671)

316 This ancient morsel, this Sir Prudence, who

Ancient morsel: "aged mere fragment of a man" (Kittredge, 39); **morsel**: "choice dish" (Orgel, 142)

317 Should not upbraid our course. For all the rest,

Should not: "would not then be able to" (Bevington, 37)

318 They'll take suggestion as a cat laps milk;

Suggestion: "evil prompting" (Riverside, 1,671); **as . . . milk**: "i.e. naturally and eagerly" (Orgel, 142)

319 They'll tell the clock to any business that

Tell . . . to: "i.e. agree that the time sorts with" (Riverside, 1,671); "say yes" (Langbaum, 73)

320 We say befits the hour.

SEBASTIAN

321 Thy case, dear friend,

322 Shall be my president; as thou got'st Milan,   **President**: "precedent"
(Riverside, 1,671)

323 I'll come by Naples. Draw thy sword: one stroke

324 Shall free thee from the tribute which thou payest;

325 And I the king shall love thee.

ANTONIO

326 Draw together;

327 And when I rear my hand, do you the like,

328 To fall it on Gonzalo.   **Fall it**: "let it fall"
(Riverside, 1,671)

SEBASTIAN

329 O, but one word.

They talk apart

Re-enter ARIEL, invisible   ***Invisible***: "implies nothing
about his costume,
but only that the other
characters cannot see
him." (Orgel, 142)

ARIEL

330 My master through his art foresees the danger   **My master . . . living**:
"Ariel acts briefly as a
chorus. The lines are
addressed not to the
sleeping Gonzalo but to
the audience." (Orgel, 142)

331 That you, his friend, are in; and sends me forth--   **His friend**: "Gonzalo"
(Kittredge, 40)

332 For else his project dies--to keep them living.   **Project**: "The word
combines the meanings
of both scheme and
purpose."; **them**: "Gonzalo
and Alonso" (Orgel, 143)

Sings in GONZALO's ear

333 While you here do snoring lie,

334 Open-eyed conspiracy

335 His time doth take.   **Time**: "opportunity"
(Riverside, 1,672)

336 If of life you keep a care,

337 Shake off slumber, and beware:

338 Awake, awake!

ANTONIO

339 Then let us both be sudden.   **Sudden**: "prompt in
action" (Kittredge, 40)

GONZALO

340 Now, good angels

341 Preserve the king.

They wake

ALONSO

342 Why, how now? ho, awake! Why are you drawn?

343 Wherefore this ghastly looking?   **Ghastly**: "full of fear
(OED 3)" (Orgel, 143)

GONZALO

344 What's the matter?

SEBASTIAN

345 Whiles we stood here securing your repose,   **Securing**: "guarding"
                                                  (Riverside, 1,672)

346 Even now, we heard a hollow burst of bellowing

347 Like bulls, or rather lions: did't not wake you?

348 It stook mine ear most terribly.   **Strook**: "struck"
                                        (Riverside, 1,672)

ALONSO

349 I heard nothing.

ANTONIO

350 O, 'twas a din to fright a monster's ear,

351 To make an earthquake! sure, it was the roar

352 Of a whole herd of lions.

ALONSO

353 Heard you this, Gonzalo?

GONZALO

354 Upon mine honor, sir, I heard a humming,   **A humming**: "Ariel's
                                                song, heard dimly in
                                                sleep" (Kittredge, 40)

355 And that a strange one too, which did awake me:

356 I shaked you, sir, and cried: as mine eyes open'd,   **Cried**: "called out"
                                                          (Riverside, 1,672)

357 I saw their weapons drawn: there was a noise,

358 That's verily. 'Tis best we stand upon our guard,   **Verily**: "the truth"
                                                   (Langbaum, 74)

359 Or that we quit this place; let's draw our weapons.

ALONSO

360 Lead off this ground; and let's make further search

361 For my poor son.

GINZALO

362 Heavens keep him from these beasts!

363 For he is, sure, i' the island.

ALONSO

364 Lead away.

ARIEL

365 Prospero my lord shall know what I have done:

366 So, king, go safely on to seek thy son.

Exeunt   *Exeunt*: "Ariel probably departs in a different direction from the rest." (Orgel, 144)

SCENE II. Another part of the island.

Enter CALIBAN with a burden of wood. A noise of thunder heard

CALIBAN

1 All the infections that the sun sucks up

Sucks up: "Pestilential mists were thought to be drawn up from bogs by the sun" (Kittredge, 41)

2 From bogs, fens, flats, on Prosper fall and make him

Flats: "swamps" (Bevington, 39)

3 By inch-meal a disease! His spirits hear me

By inch-meal: "inch by inch. Cf. *piecemeal*" (Riverside, 1,672)

4 And yet I needs must curse. But they'll nor pinch,

Needs must: "have to" (Bevington, 39); **nor**: "neither" (Bevington, 39)

5 Fright me with urchin-shows, pitch me i' the mire,

Urchin-shows: "sights of goblins in the shape of hedgehogs" (Riverside, 1,672); "impish apparitions" (Langbaum, 75)

6 Nor lead me, like a fire-brand, in the dark

Like: "in the shape of" (Kittredge, 41); **fire-brand**: "literally a piece of wood kindled at the fire; not recorded as a term for a will-o'-the-wisp. Shakespeare's use is metaphorical." (Orgel, 144)

7 Out of my way, unless he bid 'em; but

8 For every trifle are they set upon me;

9 Sometime like apes that mow and chatter at me

Mow: "make faces or grimaces" (Orgel, 144)

10 And after bite me, then like hedgehogs which   **Like hedgehogs**: "the
urchin-shows of l. 5"
(Orgel, 144)

11 Lie tumbling in my barefoot way and mount   **Mount**: "raise"
(Kittredge, 42)

12 Their pricks at my footfall; sometime am I   **Pricks**: "quills (of the
hedgehog or porcupine)"
(Kittredge, 42)

13 All wound with adders who with cloven tongues   **Wound**: "twined about"
(Riverside, 1,672)

14 Do hiss me into madness.

Enter TRINCULO   ***Trinculo***: "the name
is related to Italian
trincare, drink deeply,
and *trincone*, a drunkard."
(Orgel, 145)

15 Lo, now, lo!

16 Here comes a spirit of his, and to torment me

17 For bringing wood in slowly. I'll fall flat;

18 Perchance he will not mind me.   **Mind**: "notice"
(Riverside, 1,672)

TRINCULO

19 Here's neither bush nor shrub, to bear off   **Bear off**: "ward off"
(Riverside, 1,672)

20 any weather at all, and another storm brewing;

21 I hear it sing i' the wind: yond same black

22 cloud, yond huge one, looks like a foul   **Foul bombard**: "dirty
leather jug" (Bevington, 40)

23 bumbard that would shed his liquor. If it   **His**: "its" (Bevington, 40)

24 should thunder as it did before, I know not

25 where to hide my head: yond same cloud cannot

26 choose but fall by pailfuls. What have we

27 here? a man or a fish? dead or alive? A fish:

28 he smells like a fish; a very ancient and fish-

29 like smell; a kind of not of the newest Poor-   **Poor-John**: "cheap dried fish" (Riverside, 1,672)

30 John. A strange fish! Were I in England now,

31 as once I was, and had but this fish painted,   **Painted**: "i.e. on a sign hung outside a booth at a fair to attract customers, with the monster exhibited within" (Riverside, 1,672)

32 not a holiday fool there but would give a piece   **Holiday fool**: "one at a fair, where such 'side shows' were common" (Kittredge, 42)

33 of silver: there would this monster make a   **Make a man**: "make a man's fortune, with obvious punning sense 'be indistinguishable from an Englishman'" (Riverside, 1,672)

34 man; any strange beast there makes a man:

35 when they will not give a doit to relieve a lame   **Doit**: "a coin of small value, originally equivalent to half a farthing" (Orgel, 145)

36 beggar, they will lazy out ten to see a dead

A dead Indian: "The display of New-World natives, living and dead, had been a popular and lucrative enterprise since the early sixteenth century." (Orgel, 145)

37 Indian. Legged like a man and his fins like

38 arms! Warm o' my troth! I do now let loose

O' my troth: "by my faith" (Riverside, 1,672)

39 my opinion; hold it no longer: this is no fish,

Hold it: "hold it back" (Riverside, 1,672)

40 but an islander, that hath lately suffered by a

Suffered: "perished" (Orgel, 145)

41 thunderbolt.

Thunder

42 Alas, the storm is come again! my best way is to

43 creep under his gaberdine; there is no other

Gaberdine: "cloak of coarse cloth" (Orgel, 145)

44 shelter hereabouts: misery acquaints a man with

45 strange bed-fellows. I will here shroud till the

Shroud: "take shelter" (Bevington, 40)

46 dregs of the storm be past.

Dregs: "lees (recurring to the image of the rain as liquor poured from a jug)" (Riverside, 1,672)

Enter STEPHANO, singing: a bottle in his hand

STEPHANO

47 I shall no more to sea, to sea,

48 Here shall I die ashore--

49 This is a very scurvy tune to sing at a man's

50 funeral: well, here's my comfort. *(Drinks)*

51 *(Sings)* The master, the swabber, the boatswain and I,

Swabber: "seaman who cleans the decks" (Orgel, 146)

52 The gunner and his mate

53 Loved Mall, Meg and Marian and Margery,

Mall: "a diminutive form of 'Mary'" (Kittredge, 43)

54 But none of us cared for Kate;

55 For she had a tongue with a tang,

Tang: "sting; originally 'the tongue of a serpent, formerly thought to be a stinging organ' (OED)." (Orgel, 146)

56 Would cry to a sailor, Go hang!

57 She loved not the savor of tar nor of pitch,

58 Yet a tailor might scratch her where'er she did itch:

Tailor: "Tailors were conventionally supposed to be unmanly"; **scratch ... itch**: "implying the gratification of sensual desire" (Orgel, 146); **tailor ... itch**: "(A dig at tailors for their supposed effeminacy and a bawdy suggestion of satisfying a sexual craving.)" (Bevington, 41)

59 Then to sea, boys, and let her go hang!

60 This is a scurvy tune too: but here's my comfort. *(Drinks)*

CALIBAN

61 Do not torment me: Oh!

Do . . . me: "Caliban takes Stephano for a spirit sent by Prospero to plague him" (Riverside, 1,673)

STEPHANO

62 What's the matter? Have we devils here? Do you put

What's the matter: "What's going on?" (Orgel, 146)

63 tricks upon 's with salvages and men of Inde, ha? I

Put tricks upon 's:" "delude us with a conjuror's or showman's devices"; **salvages**: "savages"; **Inde**: "India" (Riverside, 1,673); **men of Inde**: "Indians" (Kittredge, 43)

64 have not scaped drowning to be afeard now of your

65 four legs; for it hath been said, As proper a man as

As . . . legs: "Stephano adapts a proverbial expression by substituting *four* for *two*. *Proper* = handsome" (Riverside, 1,673)

66 ever went on four legs cannot make him give ground;

67 and it shall be said so again while Stephano

68 breathes at' nostrils.

At': "at the" (Riverside, 1,673)

CALIBAN

69 The spirit torments me; Oh!

STEPHANO

70 This is some monster of the isle with four legs, who

71 hath got, as I take it, an ague. Where the devil

> **Ague**: "Commonly used for the shivering stage of fever, hence any fit of shaking or quaking, as Caliban is doing under his gabardine."
> (Orgel, 147)

72 should he learn our language? I will give him some

> **Should he learn**: "could he have learned" (Bevington, 41)

73 relief, if it be but for that. if I can recover him

> **For that**: "i.e. because he knows our language"; **recover**: "restore" (Riverside, 1,673)

74 and keep him tame and get to Naples with him, he's a

75 present for any emperor that ever trod on neat's-leather.

> **Present**: "dwarfs and misshapen creatures were often maintained at court or great houses as fools or fantastic attendants"; **ever . . . leather**: "ever walked in a cowhide shoe (a proverbial expression)" (Kittredge, 44); **neat's-leather**: "cowhide" (Riverside, 1,673)

CALIBAN

76 Do not torment me, prithee; I'll bring my wood home faster.

STEPHANO

77 He's in his fit now and does not talk after the

> **Fit**: "delirium" (Kittredge, 44); **after the wisest**: "in

the wisest fashion"
(Orgel, 147)

78 wisest. He shall taste of my bottle: if he have

79 never drunk wine afore will go near to remove his **Afore**: "before"
(Bevington, 42); **go near to**: "do much to" (Orgel, 147); "nearly" (Bevington, 42)

80 fit. If I can recover him and keep him tame, I will **I will . . . much**: "whatever I can take for him won't be too much" (Riverside, 1,673); **recover**: "restore" (Bevington, 42)

81 not take too much for him; he shall pay for him that **He shall . . . hath him**: "i.e., anyone who wants him will have to pay dearly for him" (Bevington, 42)

82 hath him, and that soundly. **Hath**: "gets" (Riverside, 1,673)

CALIBAN

83 Thou dost me yet but little hurt; thou wilt anon, I **Thou wilt anon**: "i.e. you will hurt me more very soon" (Riverside, 1,673)

84 know it by thy trembling: now Prosper works upon thee. **Thy trembling**: "Trinculo is now quaking with fear." (Orgel, 147)

STEPHANO

85 Come on your ways; open your mouth; here is that

86 which will give language to you, cat: open your

Cat: "(alluding to the proverb 'Liquor will make a cat talk')" (Langbaum, 78)

87 mouth; this will shake your shaking, I can tell you,

88 and that soundly: you cannot tell who's your friend:

You . . . friend: "Presumably Caliban dislikes his first taste." (Orgel, 147)

89 open your chaps again.

Chaps: "jaws" (Riverside, 1,673)

TRINCULO

90 I should know that voice: it should be--but he is

91 drowned; and these are devils: O defend me!

STEPHANO

92 Four legs and two voices: a most delicate monster!

Delicate: "ingenious" (Riverside, 1,673); "exquisitely made" (Orgel, 147)

93 His forward voice now is to speak well of his

94 friend; his backward voice is to utter foul speeches

95 and to detract. If all the wine in my bottle will

Detract: "backbite, slander" (Kittredge, 44); **if . . . him**: "if it takes all the wine in my bottle to cure him" (Orgel, 148)

96 recover him, I will help his ague. Come. Amen! I

Help: "cure" (Bevington, 42)

97 will pour some in thy other mouth.

TRINCULO

98 Stephano!

STEPHANO

99 Doth thy other mouth call me? Mercy, mercy! This is

Call me: "speak my name (implying supernatural knowledge)" (Orgel, 148)

100 a devil, and no monster: I will leave him; I have no

101 long spoon.

Long spoon: "alluding to the proverb 'He must have a long spoon that will eat with the devil.'" (Riverside, 1,673)

TRINCULO

102 Stephano! If thou beest Stephano, touch me and

103 speak to me: for I am Trinculo--be not afeard--thy

104 good friend Trinculo.

STEPHANO

105 If thou beest Trinculo, come forth: I'll pull thee

106 by the lesser legs: if any be Trinculo's legs,

107 these are they. Thou art very Trinculo indeed! How

108 camest thou to be the siege of this moon-calf? Can

Siege: "excrement"; **moon-calf**: "monstrosity, creature born mis-shapen because of lunar influence" (Riverside, 1,673)

114

109 he vent Trinculos?

Vent: "emit"
(Riverside, 1,673);
"defecate"
(Orgel, 148)

TRINCULO

110 I took him to be killed with a thunder-stroke. But

111 art thou not drowned, Stephano? I hope now thou art

112 not drowned. Is the storm overblown? I hid me

Overblown: "blown
over" (Bevington, 43)

113 under the dead moon-calf's gaberdine for fear of

114 the storm. And art thou living, Stephano? O

115 Stephano, two Neapolitans 'scaped!

STEPHANO

116 Prithee, do not turn me about; my stomach is not constant.

Turn me about:
"Presumably
Stephano, in his
relief, is attempting
a kind of dance with
Trinculo." (Orgel,
148); **constant**:
"settled, steady"
(Kittredge, 45)

CALIBAN

117 [Aside] These be fine things, and if they be

And if: "if"
(Riverside, 1,673)

118 not sprites.

119 That's a brave god and bears celestial liquor.

**That's a brave
god**: "Caliban's
reaction to Stephano
parallels Miranda's

to Ferdinand ('a thing divine') and Ferdinand's to Miranda ('most sure, the goddess . . . '), I.2.491 ff." (Orgel, 149); **brave**: "magnificent" (Kittredge, 45); **bears**: "he carries" (Bevington, 43)

120 I will kneel to him.

STEPHANO

121 How didst thou 'scape? How camest thou hither?

122 swear by this bottle how thou camest hither. I

123 escaped upon a butt of sack which the sailors

Butt of sack: "barrel of Spanish wine" (Riverside, 1,673); "a generic term for sherry and similar wines" (Kittredge, 45)

124 heaved o'erboard, by this bottle; which I made of

By this bottle: "I swear by this bottle" (Bevington, 43)

125 the bark of a tree with mine own hands since I was

Since: "after" (Bevington, 43)

126 cast ashore.

CALIBAN

127 I'll swear upon that bottle to be thy true subject;

128 for the liquor is not earthly.

STEPHANO

129 Here; swear then how thou escaped'st.

Here . . . escaped'st: "Stephano ignores Caliban until l. 136." (Orgel, 149)

TRINCULO

130 Swom ashore. man, like a duck: I can swim like a

Swom: "swam" (Riverside, 1,673)

131 duck, I'll be sworn.

STEPHANO

132 Here, kiss the book. Though thou canst swim like a

Kiss the book: "Trinculo has taken his oath on the bottle, not on the customary Bible. Stephano means 'Take a drink.'" (Riverside, 1,673)

133 duck, thou art made like a goose.

Goose: "Referring to Trinculo's posture as he drinks; but also, the term was a byword for giddiness and unsteadiness on the feet." (Orgel, 149)

TRINCULO

134 O Stephano. hast any more of this?

STEPHANO

135 The whole butt, man: my cellar is in a rock by the

136 sea-side where my wine is hid. How now, moon-calf!

137 how does thine ague?

Donald J. Richardson

CALIBAN

138 Hast thou not dropp'd from heaven?

STEPHANO

139 Out o' the moon, I do assure thee: I was the man i'

140 the moon when time was.

When time was: "once upon a time" (Riverside, 1,673)

CALIBAN

141 I have seen thee in her and I do adore thee:

142 My mistress show'd me thee and thy dog and thy bush.

Dog . . . bush: "the man in the moon was placed there in punishment for gathering firewood on Sunday." (Riverside, 1,673)

STEPHANO

143 Come, swear to that; kiss the book: I will furnish

144 it anon with new contents swear.

TRINCULO

145 By this good light, this is a very shallow monster!

This good light: "i.e. the sun" (Orgel, 150); **shallow**: "silly" (Kittredge, 46)

146 I afeard of him! A very weak monster! The man i'

147 the moon! A most poor credulous monster! Well

Well drawn: "That's a good long draught you've taken" (Riverside, 1,673)

148 drawn, monster, in good sooth!

Sooth: "truth"
(Riverside, 1,673)

CALIBAN

149 I'll show thee every fertile inch o' th' island;

150 And I will kiss thy foot: I prithee, be my god.

TRINCULO

151 By this light, a most perfidious and drunken

152 monster! when 's god's asleep, he'll rob his bottle.

When . . . bottle:
"i.e., Caliban wouldn't
even stop at robbing
his god of his bottle
if he could catch him
asleep" (Bevington, 44)
CALIBAN

153 I'll kiss thy foot; I'll swear myself thy subject.

STEPHANO

154 Come on then; down, and swear.

TRINCULO

155 I shall laugh myself to death at this puppy-headed

156 monster. A most scurvy monster! I could find in my

157 heart to beat him,--

STEPHANO

158 Come, kiss.

TRINCULO

159 But that the poor monster's in drink: an abominable monster! **In drink**:
"drunk"
(Bevington, 44)

CALIBAN

160 I'll show thee the best springs; I'll pluck thee berries;

161 I'll fish for thee and get thee wood enough.

162 A plague upon the tyrant that I serve! **Tyrant**:
"oppressive
usurper"
(Kittredge, 46)

163 I'll bear him no more sticks, but follow thee,

164 Thou wondrous man.

TRINCULO

165 A most ridiculous monster, to make a wonder of a

166 Poor drunkard!

CALIBAN

167 I prithee, let me bring thee where crabs grow; **Crabs**: "crab apples"
(Riverside, 1,674)

168 And I with my long nails will dig thee pig-nuts; **Pig-nuts**: "peanuts"
(Riverside, 1,674);
"earthnuts—
underground tubers
of a certain plant
which have a nutty
taste" (Kittredge, 46-
7)

169 Show thee a jay's nest and instruct thee how

170 To snare the nimble marmozet; I'll bring thee

Marmozet: "marmoset (a small monkey)" (Riverside, 1,674)

171 To clustering filberts and sometimes I'll get thee

Filberts: "hazelnuts" (Orgel, 151)

172 Young scamels from the rock. Wilt thou go with me?

Scamels: "Meaning unknown, but apparently either shellfish or rock-inhabiting birds. Some editors emend to *sea-mels*, i.e. sea-mews." (Riverside, 1,674)

STEPHANO

173 I prithee now, lead the way without any more

174 talking. Trinculo, the king and all our company

175 else being drowned, we will inherit here: here;

Else: "in addition, besides ourselves" (Bevington, 45); **inherit:** "take possession" (Kittredge, 47)

176 bear my bottle: fellow Trinculo, we'll fill him by

Him: "either Caliban, or conceivably the bottle being personified" (Orgel, 151)

177 and by again.

CALIBAN

178 [Sings drunkenly] Farewell master; farewell, farewell!

TRINCULO

179 A howling monster: a drunken monster!

CALIBAN

180 No more dams I'll make for fish

Dams: "(to catch fish and keep them)" (Langbaum, 81)

181 Nor fetch in firing

Firing: "firewood" (Orgel, 151)

182 At requiring;

183 Nor scrape trenchering, nor wash dish

Trenchering: "trenchers, wooden plates" (Riverside, 1,674)

184 'Ban, 'Ban, Cacaliban

'Ban: "abbreviating Caliban" (Orgel, 151)

185 Has a new master: get a new man.

186 Freedom, high-day! high-day, freedom! freedom,

High-day: "holiday"; **get a new man**: "addressed to the old master, Prospero" (Orgel, 151)

187 hey-day, freedom!

STEPHANO

188 O brave monster! Lead the way.

Brave: "fine" (Kittredge, 48)

Exeunt

ACT III

SCENE I. Before PROSPERO'S Cell.

Enter FERDINAND, bearing a log

FERDINAND

1 There be some sports are painful, and their labor

> **Sports**: "pastimes, activities" (Bevington, 46); **are painful**: "that are laborious"; **their . . . off**: "their laboriousness increases our pleasure in them (?) or our pleasure in them offsets their laboriousness (?)" (Riverside, 1,674)

2 Delight in them sets off: some kinds of baseness

> **Sets off**: "cancels" (Langbaum, 81); **baseness**: "menial activity" (Riverside, 1,674)

3 Are nobly undergone and most poor matters

> **Undergone**: "undertaken" (Bevington, 46); **most poor**: "poorest" (Orgel, 152)

4 Point to rich ends. This my mean task

> **Mean**: "lowly" (Orgel, 152)

5 Would be as heavy to me as odious, but

> **But**: "except that" (Orgel, 152)

6 The mistress which I serve quickens what's dead

> **Quickens**: "brings to life" (Riverside, 1,674); **what's dead**: "i.e. his deadly labor" (Kittredge, 49)

Donald J. Richardson

7 And makes my labors pleasures: O, she is

8 Ten times more gentle than her father's crabbed,

9 And he's composed of harshness. I must remove

10 Some thousands of these logs and pile them up,

11 Upon a sore injunction: my sweet mistress

Sore injunction: "harsh command" (Riverside, 1,674)

12 Weeps when she sees me work, and says, such baseness

Such . . . executor: "Such base labor was never performed by one so noble" (Orgel, 152)

13 Had never like executor. I forget:

Had . . . executor: "i.e., was never before undertaken by one of my noble rank" (Bevington, 46); **like:** "such, i.e. such a noble" (Riverside, 1,674); **I forget:** "i.e. to work at my task" (Orgel, 152)

14 But these sweet thoughts do even refresh my labors,

15 Most busy lest, when I do it.

Most . . . it: "when I am working hardest" (Riverside, 1,674)

Enter MIRANDA; and PROSPERO at a distance, unseen

MIRANDA

16 Alas, now, pray you,

17 Work not so hard: I would the lightning had

18 Burnt up those logs that you are enjoin'd to pile!   **Enjoin'd**: "commanded" (Bevington, 46)

19 Pray, set it down and rest you: when this burns,   **This**: "i.e., the log" (Bevington, 46)

20 'Twill weep for having wearied you. My father   **Weep**: "i.e. exude resin" (Riverside, 1,674)

21 Is hard at study; pray now, rest yourself;

22 He's safe for these three hours.   **He's safe**: "i.e. we are safe from him" (Orgel, 153); **these**: "i.e., the next" (Bevington, 46)

FERDINAND

23 O most dear mistress,

24 The sun will set before I shall discharge   **Discharge**: "fullfil" (Kittredge, 50)

25 What I must strive to do.

MIRANDA

26 If you'll sit down,

27 I'll bear your logs the while: pray, give me that;

28 I'll carry it to the pile.

FERDINAND

29 No, precious creature;

30 I had rather crack my sinews, break my back,

31 Than you should such dishonor undergo,

32 While I sit lazy by.

Donald J. Richardson

MIRANDA

33 It would become me

34 As well as it does you: and I should do it

35 With much more ease; for my good will is to it,

36 And yours it is against.

PROSPERO

37 Poor worm, thou art infected!

> **Worm**: "any small creature" (Orgel, 153)

38 This visitation shows it.

> **Visitation**: "(1) visit of the sick (2) visitation of the plague, i.e., infection of love" (Bevington, 47)

MIRANDA

39 You look wearily.

FERDINAND

40 No, noble mistress; 'tis fresh morning with me

> **'Tis fresh . . . night**: "even at night, when I am very tired, your presence makes me feel as unwearied as I do in the morning" (Kittredge, 51)

41 When you are by at night. I do beseech you--

> **When . . . night**: "The language is purely conventional: Ferdinand has not yet passed a night since meeting Miranda." (Orgel, 153); **by**: "nearby" (Bevington, 47)

42 Chiefly that I might set it in my prayers--

43 What is your name?

MIRANDA

44 Miranda.--O my father,

45 I have broke your hest to say so!

> **Hest**: "command"
> (Riverside, 1,674)

FERDINAND

46 Admir'd Miranda!

> **Admir'd Miranda**: "a
> pun, since *Miranda* =
> admired, i.e. wondered at"
> (Riverside, 1,674); "the
> Latin 'Miranda' means
> 'wonderful'"
> (Langbaum, 83)

47 Indeed the top of admiration! worth

48 What's dearest to the world! Full many a lady

> **Dearest**: "most valuable"
> (Orgel, 154)

49 I have eyed with best regard and many a time

> **Best regard**: "highest
> approval" (Riverside, 1,674)

50 The harmony of their tongues hath into bondage

51 Brought my too diligent ear: for several virtues

> **Diligent**: "attentive (OED
> 3)" (Orgel, 154); **several**:
> "particular" (Riverside,
> 1,674); **virtues**:
> "admirable qualities"
> (Kittredge, 51)

52 Have I liked several women; never any

> **Several**: "various,
> different" (Orgel, 154)

53 With so fun soul, but some defect in her

54 Did quarrel with the noblest grace she ow'd

Noblest grace: "finest quality" (Kittredge, 51); **ow'd**: "owned" (Riverside, 1,674)

55 And put it to the foil: but you, O you,

Put it to the foil: "(1) overthrew in (as in wrestling) (2) served as a *foil*, or contrast, to set it off" (Bevington, 47)

56 So perfect and so peerless, are created

57 Of every creature's best!

Of: "out of" (Bevington, 48); **creature**: "created being" (Orgel, 154)

MIRANDA

58 I do not know

59 One of my sex; no woman's face remember,

60 Save, from my glass, mine own; nor have I seen

61 More that I may call men than you, good friend,

62 And my dear father: how features are abroad,

How . . . of: "I do not know what people look like elsewhere" (Orgel, 154); **abroad**: "out in the world, away from home" (Kittredge, 51)

63 I am skilless of; but, by my modesty,

Skilless: "ignorant" (Riverside, 1,675); **modesty**: "virginity" (Orgel, 154)

64 The jewel in my dower, I would not wish

Dower: "(here) dowry" (Orgel, 154)

65 Any companion in the world but you,

66 Nor can imagination form a shape,

67 Besides yourself, to like of. But I prattle

Like of: "to be pleased with" (Kittredge, 51)

68 Something too wildly and my father's precepts

Something: "somewhat" (Bevington, 48)

69 I therein do forget.

FERDINAND

70 I am in my condition

Condition: "rank" (Riverside, 1,675)

71 A prince, Miranda; I do think, a king;

72 I would not so!--and would no more endure

Would not: "wish it were not" (Orgel, 154)

73 This wooden slavery than to suffer

Wooden slavery: "being compelled to carry wood" (Riverside, 1,675)

74 The flesh-fly blow my mouth. Hear my soul speak:

Flesh-fly: "fly that deposits its eggs in dead flesh" (Orgel, 155); **blow**: "defile" (Riverside, 1,675)

75 The very instant that I saw you, did

76 My heart fly to your service; there resides,

77 To make me slave to it; and for your sake

78 Am I this patient log-man.

MIRANDA

79 Do you love me?

FERDINAND

80 O heaven, O earth, bear witness to this sound

81 And crown what I profess with kind event

Kind event: "favorable outcome" (Riverside, 1,675)

82 If I speak true! if hollowly, invert

Hollowly: "insincerely"; **invert . . . to mischief**: "turn . . . to ill fortune" (Riverside, 1,675)

83 What best is boded me to mischief! I

Boded: "destined" (Riverside, 1,675); **mischief**: "disaster" (Kittredge, 52)

84 Beyond all limit of what else i' the world

What: "whatever (Abbott 254)" (Orgel, 155)

85 Do love, prize, honor you.

MIRANDA

86 I am a fool

87 To weep at what I am glad of.

PROSPERO

88 Fair encounter

Fair encounter: "fortunate meeting" (Kittredge, 52)

89 Of two most rare affections! Heavens rain grace

Rare affections: "dispositions (or characters) of rarest quality" (Kittredge, 52)

90 On that which breeds between 'em!

**On that ... between
'em**: "on the love which
comes into being as a
result of this association"
(Kittredge, 52)

FERDINAND

91 Wherefore weep you?

MIRANDA

92 At mine unworthiness that dare not offer

**That dare ...
cunning**: "The *offer* is
unconsciously sexual; with
this is trifling Miranda
realizes her indiscretion,
acknowledges the
bashful cunning (96)
of her language, and
undertakes to confront its
implications." (Orgel, 155)

93 What I desire to give, and much less take

94 What I shall die to want. But this is trifling;

Die: "(probably with
an unconscious sexual
meaning that underlies all
of ll. 92-96)" (Bevington,
49); **want**: "be without"
(Riverside, 1,675);
trifling: "i.e., to speak
in riddles like this"
(Langbaum, 84)

95 And all the more it seeks to hide itself,

It: "her love" (Kittredge, 52)

96 The bigger bulk it shows. Hence, bashful cunning!

Bashful cunning:
"coyness" (Riverside,
1,675)

97 And prompt me, plain and holy innocence!

98 I am your wife, if you will marry me;

99 If not, I'll die your maid: to be your fellow	**Maid**: "handmaiden" **fellow**: "mate" (Riverside, 1,675); "equal" (Langbaum, 85)
100 You may deny me; but I'll be your servant,	
101 Whether you will or no.	**Will**: "desire it" (Bevington, 49)

FERDINAND

102 My mistress, dearest;	**Mistress**: "'a woman who has command over a man's heart' (OED 10), in this context without illicit overtones" (Orgel, 156)
103 And I thus humble ever.	

MIRANDA

104 My husband, then?

FERDINAND

105 Ay, with a heart as willing	**Willing**: "desirous (OED 1)" (Orgel, 156)
106 As bondage e'er of freedom: here's my hand.	**Of freedom**: "i.e., to win freedom" (Langbaum, 85); **my hand . . . in't**: "'with heart and hand' is proverbial (Tilley H 339)" (Orgel, 156)

MIRANDA

107 And mine, with my heart in't; and now farewell

108 Till half an hour hence.

FERDINAND

109 A thousand thousand!

Thousand: "i.e. thousand farewells" (Riverside, 1,675); "i.e. a million" (Orgel, 156)

Exeunt FERDINAND and MIRANDA severally

PROSPERO

110 So glad of this as they I cannot be,

111 Who are surprised withal; but my rejoicing

Surprised: "both astonished and caught unawares" (Orgel, 156); **withal**: "with it, i.e. by it" (Riverside, 1,675)

112 At nothing can be more. I'll to my book,

113 For yet ere supper-time must I perform

114 Much business appertaining.

Appertaining: "related to this" (Bevington, 49)

Exit

SCENE II. Another part of the island.

Enter CALIBAN, STEPHANO, and TRINCULO

STEPHANO

1 Tell not me; when the butt is out, we will drink

Tell not me: "Trinculo has been trying to moderate their drinking" (Orgel, 156); **out**: "empty" (Riverside, 1,675)

2 water; not a drop before: therefore bear up, and

Bear ... 'em: "stand firm and attack. Stephano uses naval jargon as an encouragement to drink." (Riverside, 1,675)

3 board 'em. Servant-monster, drink to me.

TRINCULO

4 Servant-monster! the folly of this island! They

Folly of: "low level of intellect on" (Riverside, 1,675)

5 say there's but five upon this isle: we are three

6 of them; if th' other two be brained like us, the

Be brained like us: "i.e. are no more intelligent than we are" (Orgel, 157)

7 state totters.

STEPHANO

8 Drink, servant-monster, when I bid thee: thy eyes

9 are almost set in thy head.

Set: "sunk out of sight. Trinculo puns on the sense 'placed.'" (Riverside, 1,675); "fixed (drunkenly)" (Orgel, 157)

TRINCULO

10 Where should they be set else? he were a brave

Set: "fixed in a drunken stare; or sunk, like the sun" (Bevington, 50); **brave**: "fine" (Kittredge, 54)

11 monster indeed, if they were set in his tail.

Set: "placed" (Bevington, 50)

STEPHANO

12 My man-monster hath drown'd his tongue in sack:

13 for my part, the sea cannot drown me; I swam, ere I

14 could recover the shore, five and thirty leagues off   **Recover**: "reach"
(Kittredge, 54); **five and
thirty leagues**: "a league
was a variable measure,
usually about 3 miles;
hence Stephano is claiming
to have swum over 100
miles"; **off and on**: "either
one way and another, or
intermittently" (Orgel, 157)

15 and on. By this light, thou shalt be my lieutenant,   **By this light**: "(An oath:
by the light of the sun.)"
(Bevington, 50)

16 monster, or my standard.   **Standard**: "standard-
bearer, ensign (pun
since Caliban is so
drunk he cannot stand)"
(Langbaum, 86)

TRINCULO

17 Your lieutenant, if you list; he's no standard.   **If you list**: "if it please
you (with pun on 'list' as
pertaining to a ship that
leans over to one side)"
(Langbaum, 86)l; **no
standard**: "i.e. unable to
stand" (Riverside, 1,675)

STEPHANO

18 We'll not run, Monsieur Monster.   **Run**: "(1) retreat (2)
urinate (taking Trinculo's
standard, l. 17, in the
old sense of 'conduit')"
(Bevington, 50)

TRINCULO

19 Nor go neither; but you'll lie like dogs and yet say

> **Go**: "walk"; **lie**: "(1) lie down; (2) tell lies; (3) excrete (with a backward glance at *run* in the sense 'urinate' and perhaps at *standard* in the sense 'conduit')" (Riverside, 1,675)

20 nothing neither.

STEPHANO

21 Moon-calf, speak once in thy life, if thou beest a

22 good moon-calf.

CALIBAN

23 How does thy honor? Let me lick thy shoe.

24 I'll not serve him; he's not valiant.

TRINCULO

25 Thou liest, most ignorant monster: I am in case to

> **Case**: "fit condition" (Riverside, 1,675); "prepared (i.e. drunk, and hence valiant)" (Orgel, 157)

26 justle a constable. Why, thou debosh'd fish thou,

> **Justle**: "jostle" (Langbaum, 86); **debosh'd**: "debauched" (Riverside, 1,675)

27 was there ever man a coward that hath drunk so much

28 sack as I to-day? Wilt thou tell a monstrous lie,

> **Sack**: "Spanish white wine" (Bevington, 51)

29 being but half a fish and half a monster?

CALIBAN

30 Lo, how he mocks me! wilt thou let him, my lord?

TRINCULO

31 "Lord" quoth he! That a monster should be such a natural!

Natural: "idiot. The point is that a monster is by definition 'unnatural.'" (Riverside, 1,675)

CALIBAN

32 Lo, lo, again! bite him to death, I prithee.

STEPHANO

33 Trinculo, keep a good tongue in your head: if you

34 prove a mutineer,--the next tree! The poor monster's

The next tree: "i.e. to serve as a gallows" (Orgel, 158); "i.e., you will be hanged" (Langbaum, 87)

35 my subject and he shall not suffer indignity.

CALIBAN

36 I thank my noble lord. Wilt thou be pleased to

37 hearken once again to the suit I made to thee?

STEPHANO

38 Marry, will I kneel and repeat it; I will stand,

Marry: "indeed (originally the name of the Virgin Mary used as an oath)" (Riverside, 1,675)

39 and so shall Trinculo.

Donald J. Richardson

Enter ARIEL, invisible

CALIBAN

40 As I told thee before, I am subject to a tyrant, a   **Tyrant**: "usurper"
                                                                 (Kittredge, 55)

41 sorcerer, that by his cunning hath cheated me of the island.

ARIEL

42 Thou liest.

CALIBAN

43 Thou liest, thou jesting monkey, thou: I would my

44 valiant master would destroy thee! I do not lie.

STEPHANO

45 Trinculo, if you trouble him any more in's tale, by

46 this hand, I will supplant some of your teeth.   **Supplant**: "uproot"
                                                                 (Orgel, 158)

TRINCULO

47 Why, I said nothing.

STEPHANO

48 Mum, then, and no more. Proceed.

CALIBAN

49 I say, by sorcery he got this isle;

50 From me he got it. If thy greatness will

51 Revenge it on him--for I know thou darest,

52 But this thing dare not--

This thing: "i.e. Trinculo" (Riverside, 1,676)

STEPHANO

53 That's most certain.

CALIBAN

54 Thou shalt be lord of it and I'll serve thee.

STEPHANO

55 How now shall this be compassed?

Compassed: "brought about" (Kittredge, 56)

56 Canst thou bring me to the party?

The party: "the person concerned" (Kittredge, 56)

CALIBAN

57 Yea, yea, my lord: I'll yield him thee asleep,

58 Where thou mayst knock a nail into his head.

Knock . . . head: "on the biblical model of Jael's murder of the sleeping Sisera (Judges 4:21)" (Orgel, 159)

ARIEL

59 Thou liest; thou canst not.

CALIBAN

60 What a pied ninny's this! Thou scurvy patch!

Pied . . . patch: "foolish . . . fool (from the multicolored garb of the professional fool)" (Riverside, 1,676); **scurvy patch**: "miserable fool" (Kittredge, 56)

61 I do beseech thy greatness, give him blows

62 And take his bottle from him: when that's gone

63 He shall drink nought but brine; for I'll not show him

64 Where the quick freshes are.

> **Quick freshes**: "fresh-water springs" (Riverside, 1,676)

STEPHANO

65 Trinculo, run into no further danger:

66 interrupt the monster one word further, and,

> **One word further**: "i.e., one more time" (Bevington, 52)

67 by this hand, I'll turn my mercy out o' doors

> **Turn . . . doors**: "i.e., forget about being merciful" (Bevington, 52)

68 and make a stock-fish of thee.

> **Stock-fish**: "dried cod, so stiff it had to be beaten before cooking" (Riverside, 1,676)

TRINCULO

69 Why, what did I? I did nothing. I'll go farther

70 off.

> **Off**: "away" (Bevington, 52)

STEPHANO

71 Didst thou not say he lied?

ARIEL

72 Thou liest.

STEPHANO

73 Do I so? take thou that.

Beats TRINCULO

74 As you like this, give me the lie another time.

Give me the lie: "call me a liar" (Orgel, 159)

TRINCULO

75 I did not give the lie. Out o' your

76 wits and bearing too? A pox o' your bottle!

77 this can sack and drinking do. A murrain on

Murrain: "a disease of cattle" (Riverside, 1,676); "plague" (Orgel, 159)

78 your monster, and the devil take your fingers!

CALIBAN

79 Ha, ha, ha!

STEPHANO

80 Now, forward with your tale. Prithee, stand further

Stand further off: "i.e. further than Trinculo himself has offered to stand, l. 70." (Orgel, 159)

81 off.

CALIBAN

82 Beat him enough: after a little time

83 I'll beat him too.

STEPHANO

84 Stand farther. Come, proceed.

Donald J. Richardson

CALIBAN

85 Why, as I told thee, 'tis a custom with him,   **'Tis a custom ... sleep**: "Old Hamlet's custom too, providing Claudius with a similar opportunity for murder" (Orgel, 160)

86 I' th' afternoon to sleep: there thou mayst brain him,   **There**: "then (Abbott 70)" (Orgel, 160)

87 Having first seized his books, or with a log

88 Batter his skull, or paunch him with a stake,   **Paunch**: "stab in the belly" (Riverside, 1,676)

89 Or cut his wezand with thy knife. Remember   **Wezand**: "windpipe" (Riverside, 1,676)

90 First to possess his books; for without them   **Possess**: "seize" (Kittredge, 57)

91 He's but a sot, as I am, nor hath not   **Sot**: "fool" (Riverside, 1,676)

92 One spirit to command: they all do hate him

93 As rootedly as I. Burn but his books.

94 He has brave utensils,--for so he calls them--   **Utensils**: "either magical paraphernalia or simply household goods" (Orgel, 160)

95 Which when he has a house, he'll deck withal   **Deck withal**: "furnish it with" (Kittredge, 57)

96 And that most deeply to consider is

97 The beauty of his daughter; he himself

98 Calls her a nonpareil: I never saw a woman,   **Nonpareil**: "without an equal" (Kittredge, 57)

99 But only Sycorax my dam and she;

She: "for 'her' Abbott 211"
(Orgel, 160)

100 But she as far surpasseth Sycorax

101 As great'st does least.

STEPHANO

102 Is it so brave a lass?

Brave: "handsome,
beautiful" (Kittredge, 57)

CALIBAN

103 Ay, lord; she will become thy bed, I warrant.

Become: "suit"
(Bevington, 53)

104 And bring thee forth brave brood.

STEPHANO

105 Monster, I will kill this man: his daughter and I

106 will be king and queen--save our graces!--and

107 Trinculo and thyself shall be viceroys. Dost thou

108 like the plot, Trinculo?

TRINCULO

109 Excellent.

STEPHANO

110 Give me thy hand: I am sorry I beat thee; but,

111 while thou livest, keep a good tongue in thy head.

Keep . . . head: "Stephano
repeats his proverbial
warning of l. 33."
(Orgel, 160)

CALIBAN

112 Within this half hour will he be asleep:

113 Wilt thou destroy him then?

STEPHANO

114 Ay, on mine honor.

ARIEL

115 This will I tell my master.

CALIBAN

116 Thou makest me merry; I am full of pleasure:

117 Let us be jocund: will you troll the catch

Jocund: "jovial, merry" (Bevington, 54); **troll the catch**: "sing the round" (Riverside, 1,676)

118 You taught me but while-ere?

But while-ere: "a short time ago" (Riverside, 1,676)

STEPHANO

119 At thy request, monster, I will do reason, any

Reason, any reason: "anything reasonable" (Orgel, 161)

120 reason. Come on, Trinculo, let us sing.

Sings

121 Flout 'em and scout 'em

Flout: "deride"; **scout**: "jeer at" (Riverside, 1,676)

122 And scout 'em and flout 'em

123 Thought is free.

Thought is free: "a
common proverb"
(Kittredge, 58)

CALIBAN

124 That's not the tune.

Ariel plays the tune on a tabor and pipe

Tabor: "small drum worn
at the side" (Langbaum, 90)

STEPHANO

125 What is this same?

TRINCULO

126 This is the tune of our catch, played by the picture

Picture of Nobody:
"traditional image of a
man with arms and legs
but no torso; but Trinculo
means an invisible
agency" (Riverside, 1,676)

127 of Nobody.

STEPHANO

128 If thou beest a man, show thyself in thy likeness:

129 if thou beest a devil, take't as thou list.

Take't . . . list: "do as
you please (a challenge)"
(Riverside, 1,676)

TRINCULO

130 O, forgive me my sins!

STEPHANO

131 He that dies pays all debts: I defy thee. Mercy upon us! | **Mercy upon us**: "Stephano's bravado collapses." (Orgel, 162)

CALIBAN

132 Art thou afeard?

STEPHANO

133 No, monster, not I.

CALIBAN

134 Be not afeard; the isle is full of noises, | **Noises**: "musical sounds" (Riverside, 1,676)

135 Sounds and sweet airs, that give delight and hurt not.

136 Sometimes a thousand twangling instruments | **Twangling**: "an invented word" (Riverside, 1,676); "The word is usually used pejoratively." (Orgel, 162)

137 Will hum about mine ears, and sometime voices

138 That, if I then had waked after long sleep,

139 Will make me sleep again: and then, in dreaming,

140 The clouds methought would open and show riches

141 Ready to drop upon me that, when I waked,

142 I cried to dream again. | **To dream**: "desirous of dreaming" (Bevington, 54)

STEPHANO

143 This will prove a brave kingdom to me, where I shall

Brave: "excellent" (Kittredge, 58)

144 have my music for nothing.

CALIBAN

145 When Prospero is destroyed.

STEPHANO

146 That shall be by and by: I remember the story.

By and by: "immediately" (Riverside, 1,677)

TRINCULO

147 The sound is going away; let's follow it, and

148 after do our work.

STEPHANO

149 Lead, monster; we'll follow. I would I could see

150 this taborer; he lays it on.

Lays it on: "i.e. bangs his drum" (Orgel, 163)

TRINCULO

151 Wilt come? I'll follow, Stephano.

Exeunt

SCENE III. Another part of the island.

Enter ALONSO, SEBASTIAN, ANTONIO, GONZALO, ADRIAN, FRANCISCO,
and others

GONZALO

1 By'r lakin, I can go no further, sir;

By'r lakin: "by our Ladykin, i.e. the Virgin Mary" (Riverside, 1,677)

2 My old bones ache: here's a maze trod indeed

3 Through forth-rights and meanders! By your patience,

Forth-rights and meanders: "straight and winding paths" (Langbaum, 91)

4 I needs must rest me.

Needs must: "have to" (Bevington, 55)

ALONSO

5 Old lord, I cannot blame thee,

6 Who am myself attach'd with weariness,

Attach'd: "seized; a legal metaphor" (Orgel, 163); "attacked by" (Kittredge, 60)

7 To the dulling of my spirits: sit down, and rest.

To . . . spirits: "to the point at which my spirits are dulled" (Orgel, 163); **spirits**: "vital powers" (Kittredge, 60)

8 Even here I will put off my hope and keep it

Put off: "divest myself of" (Kittredge, 60)

9 No longer for my flatterer: he is drown'd

For: "as" (Riverside, 1,677)

10 Whom thus we stray to find, and the sea mocks

11 Our frustrate search on land. Well, let him go.   **Frustrate**: "frustrated, vain, fruitless" (Kittredge, 60)

ANTONIO

12 [Aside to SEBASTIAN] I am right glad that he's so   **Right**: "very" (Bevington, 55)

13 out of hope.   **Out of hope**: "despairing, discouraged" (Bevington, 55)

14 Do not, for one repulse, forego the purpose   **For**: "because of" (Riverside, 1,677)

15 That you resolved to effect.

SEBASTIAN

16 [Aside to ANTONIO] The next advantage

17 Will we take throughly.   **Throughly**: "thoroughly" (Riverside, 1,677)

ANTONIO

18 [Aside to SEBASTIAN] Let it be to-night;

19 For, now they are oppress'd with travel, they   **Now**: "now that" (Orgel, 164); **oppress'd**: "overcome"; **travel**: "our wearisome wanderings" (Kittredge, 60)

20 Will not, nor cannot, use such vigilance   **Use**: "apply" (Bevington, 56)

21 As when they are fresh.

SEBASTIAN

22 [Aside to ANTONIO] I say, to-night: no more.

Donald J. Richardson

Solemn and strange music

ALONSO

23 What harmony is this? My good friends, hark!

GONZALO

24 Marvellous sweet music!

Enter PROSPERO above, invisible. Enter several strange Shapes, bringing in a banket; they dance about it with gentle actions of salutation; and, inviting the King, & c. to eat, they depart

Banket: "banquet, i.e. light repast" (Riverside, 1,677); "Banquet scenes in Renaissance allegory generally stood for voluptuous temptation offered to the senses, to be resisted by the truly virtuous." (Kittredge, 61)

ALONSO

25 Give us kind keepers, heavens! What were these?

Kind keepers: "guardian angels" (Riverside, 1,677)

SEBASTIAN

26 A living drollery. Now I will believe

Living drollery: "puppet show with live actors" (Riverside, 1,677)

27 That there are unicorns, that in Arabia

28 There is one tree, the phoenix' throne, one phoenix

Phoenix: "a mythical Arabian bird, said to exist only one at a time, to nest in a single tree, and to reproduce by expiring in flame and then resurrecting itself from its own ashes." (Orgel, 164)

29 At this hour reigning there.

ANTONIO

30 I'll believe both;

31 And what does else want credit, come to me,

Want credit: "lack credence" (Riverside, 1,677)

32 And I'll be sworn 'tis true: travellers ne'er did lie,

33 Though fools at home condemn 'em.

GONZALO

34 If in Naples

35 I should report this now, would they believe me?

36 If I should say, I saw such islanders--

37 For, certes, these are people of the island--

Certes: "certainly" (Riverside, 1,677)

38 Who, though they are of monstrous shape, yet, note,

Monstrous: "abnormal, unnatural" (Riverside, 1,677)

39 Their manners are more gentle-kind than of

Manners: "More inclusive in sense than in the modern use. It often means 'character,' 'moral nature'" (Kittredge, 61); **gentle-kind**: "either having the graciousness of nobility or noble-mannered" (Orgel, 165)

40 Our human generation you shall find

41 Many, nay, almost any.

PROSPERO

42 [Aside] Honest lord,   **Honest**: "honorable"
                                                 (Kittredge, 62)

43 Thou hast said well; for some of you there present

44 Are worse than devils.

ALONSO

45 I cannot too much muse   **Muse**: "wonder at"
                                                 (Riverside, 1,677)

46 Such shapes, such gesture and such sound, expressing, **Gesture**: "bearing,
                                                 demeanor"
                                                 (Kittredge, 62)

47 Although they want the use of tongue, a kind **Want**: "lack"
                                                 (Bevington, 57)

48 Of excellent dumb discourse.

PROSPERO

49 [Aside] Praise in departing.   **Praise in departing**:
                                                 "i.e. don't judge until
                                                 you see the conclusion
                                                 (proverbial)"
                                                 (Riverside, 1,677)

FRANCISCO

50 They vanish'd strangely.

SEBASTIAN

51 No matter, since

52 They have left their viands behind; for we have stomachs.

Viands: "food" (Orgel, 165); **stomachs**: "appetites" (Riverside, 1,677)

53 Will't please you taste of what is here?

ALONSO

54 Not I.

GONZALO

55 Faith, sir, you need not fear. When we were boys,

56 Who would believe that there were mountaineers

Mountaineers: "mountain-dwellers" (Orgel, 166)

57 Dew-lapp'd like bulls, whose throats had hanging at 'em

Dew-lapp'd: "with pouches of skin hanging from the neck (probably alluding to travellers' tales about goiter among Swiss mountaineers)" (Riverside, 1,677)

58 Wallets of flesh? or that there were such men

Wallets: "wattles" (Orgel, 166); **men ... breasts**: "a common travellers' tale. See *Othello*, I.iii.144-45." (Riverside, 1,677)

59 Whose heads stood in their breasts? which now we find

60 Each putter-out of five for one will bring us

Each ... one: "travellers deposited a sum of money at home to be repaid fivefold if they returned, forfeited if they did not" (Riverside, 1,677)

61 Good warrant of.

Good warrant: "assurance" (Bevington, 57)

ALONSO

62 I will stand to and feed,

Stand to: "take the risk" (Riverside, 1,677)

63 Although my last: no matter, since I feel

Although my last: "even if this were to be my last meal" (Bevington, 57)

64 The best is past. Brother, my lord the duke,

Best: "i.e. best part of life" (Riverside, 1,677)

65 Stand to and do as we.

Thunder and lightning. Enter ARIEL, like a harpy; claps his wings upon the table; and, with a quaint device, the banquet vanishes

Like a harpy: "in the shape of a harpy, a rapacious monster with the face of a woman and the wings and claws of a bird of prey"; **with ... device**: "by means of an ingenious stage mechanism" (Riverside, 1,677)

ARIEL

66 You are three men of sin, whom Destiny,

67 That hath to instrument this lower world

To instrument: "as its instrument" (Langbaum, 94)

68 And what is in't, the never-surfeited sea   **Never-surfeited**: "always hungry" (Kittredge, 63)

69 Hath caused to belch up you; and on this island

70 Where man doth not inhabit; you 'mongst men

71 Being most unfit to live. I have made you mad;

72 And even with such-like valor men hang and drown   **Such-like valor**: "i.e. the valor of madness, very different from true courage" (Riverside, 1,677)

73 Their proper selves.   **Proper**: "own" (Riverside, 1,677)

ALONSO, SEBASTIAN & c. draw their swords

74 You fools! I and my fellows

75 Are ministers of Fate: the elements,   **Ministers**: "agents, servants" (Kittredge, 63)

76 Of whom your swords are temper'd, may as well   **Whom**: "which" (Riverside, 1,678); **temper'd**: "both compounded and hardened" (Orgel, 167)

77 Wound the loud winds, or with bemock'd-at stabs   **Bemock'd-at**: "scorned" (Bevington, 58)

78 Kill the still-closing waters, as diminish   **Still-closing**: "always closing as soon as parted" (Riverside, 1,678)

79 One dowle that's in my plume: my fellow-ministers   **Dowle**: "small feather" (Riverside, 1,678); **plume**: "plumage" (Langbaum, 94)

80 Are like invulnerable. If you could hurt,

Like: "similarly"
(Riverside, 1,678); **If
you could hurt**: "even
if you could hurt us"
(Langbaum, 95)

81 Your swords are now too massy for your strengths

Massy: "heavy"
(Orgel, 167)

82 And will not be uplifted. But remember--

83 For that's my business to you--that you three

84 From Milan did supplant good Prospero;

85 Exposed unto the sea, which hath requit it,

Requit: "repaid the act
(by casting you up here)"
(Riverside, 1,678)

86 Him and his innocent child: for which foul deed

87 The powers, delaying, not forgetting, have

Delaying not forgetting:
"The vengeance of the
gods is slow but sure."
(Kittredge, 64)

88 Incensed the seas and shores, yea, all the creatures,

Incensed: "roused";
the creatures: "created
things" (Kittredge, 64)

89 Against your peace. Thee of thy son, Alonso,

90 They have bereft; and do pronounce by me:

91 Lingering perdition, worse than any death

Lingering perdition:
"slow and continuous
destruction; a protracted
hell-on-earth" (Orgel, 168)

92 Can be at once, shall step by step attend

93 You and your ways; whose wraths to guard you from-- **Whose**: "i.e. those of the 'pow'rs' of line 87" (Riverside, 1,678)

94 Which here, in this most desolate isle, else falls **Else**: "otherwise" (Bevington, 58)

95 Upon your heads--is nothing but heart's sorrow **Is . . . sorrow**: "there is no means except repentance" (Riverside, 1,678)

96 And a clear life ensuing. **Clear**: "sinless" (Riverside, 1,678)

He vanishes in thunder; then, to soft music enter the Shapes again, and dance, with mocks and mows, and carrying out the table **Mocks and mows**: "mocking gestures and grimaces" (Riverside, 1,678)

PROSPERO

97 Bravely the figure of this harpy hast thou **Bravely**: "finely, elegantly" (Kittredge, 64)

98 Perform'd, my Ariel; a grace it had, devouring: **Devouring**: "i.e. making the banquet disappear" (Riverside, 1,678)

99 Of my instruction hast thou nothing bated **Bated**: "omitted" (Riverside, 1,678)

100 In what thou hadst to say: so, with good life **So**: "in the same way"; **with good life**: "Prospero praises the spirits for both vitality and naturalness in their performance." (Orgel, 168)

101 And observation strange, my meaner ministers | **Observation strange**: "exceptional care"; **meaner**: "i.e. inferior to Ariel" (Riverside, 1,678)

102 Their several kinds have done. My high charms work | **Several kinds**: "individual parts" (Riverside, 1,678)

103 And these mine enemies are all knit up | **Knit ... distractions**: "entangled in their madness" (Riverside, 1,678)

104 In their distractions; they now are in my power;

105 And in these fits I leave them, while I visit

106 Young Ferdinand, whom they suppose is drown'd,

107 And his and mine loved darling.

Exit above

GONZALO

108 I' the name of something holy, sir, why stand you | **Why ... stare**: "Gonzalo has not heard Ariel's speech" (Riverside, 1,678)

109 In this strange stare? | **Stare**: "'a condition of amazement, horror, admiration, etc., indicated by staring' (OED, sb.2 2)" (Orgel, 169)

ALONSO

110 O, it is monstrous, monstrous: | **It**: "i.e., my sin (also in l. 111)" (Bevington, 59)

111 Methought the billows spoke and told me of it;

Billows: "waves"
(Bevington, 59)

112 The winds did sing it to me, and the thunder,

113 That deep and dreadful organ-pipe, pronounced

114 The name of Prosper: it did bass my trespass.

Bass: "bass, i.e. utter in a deep voice"
(Riverside, 1,678)

115 Therefore my son i' the ooze is bedded, and

Therefore: "therefor, i.e. in consequence of his trespass" (Riverside, 1,678); **ooze**: "sea mud" (Kittredge, 65)

116 I'll seek him deeper than e'er plummet sounded

Plummet: "a lead weight attached to a line for testing depth"; **sounded**: "probed, tested the depth of" (Bevington, 59)

117 And with him there lie mudded.

Exit

SEBASTIAN

118 But one fiend at a time,

119 I'll fight their legions o'er.

O'er: "one after another" (Riverside, 1,678)

ANTONIO

120 I'll be thy second.

Exeunt SEBASTIAN, and ANTONIO

GONZALO

121 All three of them are desperate: their great guilt,

Desperate: "(a) in despair; (b) dangerously reckless" (Orgel, 169)

122 Like poison given to work a great time after,

Like poison: "Certain poisons, it was believed, did not begin to work upon the system until weeks or even months after they were administered. Thus, the poisoner might escape suspicion" (Kittredge, 65)

123 Now 'gins to bite the spirits. I do beseech you

'Gins . . . spirits: "begins to cause mental anguish" (Riverside, 1,678); **spirits**: "vital powers" (Orgel, 169)

124 That are of suppler joints, follow them swiftly

125 And hinder them from what this ecstasy

Ecstasy: "fit of madness" (Riverside, 1,678)

126 May now provoke them to.

Provoke: "prompt, instigate" (Kittredge, 65)

ADRIAN

127 Follow, I pray you.

Exeunt

ACT IV

SCENE I. Before PROSPERO'S cell.

Enter PROSPERO, FERDINAND, and MIRANDA

PROSPERO

1 If I have too austerely punish'd you,

Austerely: "harshly, rigorously" (Orgel, 170)

2 Your compensation makes amends, for I

3 Have given you here a third of mine own life,

A third life: "Various explanations have been put forward: for example, that the other two parts have been his dukedom and his books, or his late wife and his personal interests; or that Miranda represents his future, the other two parts being his past and his present; or that he has spent a third of his life on Miranda's education." (Riverside, 1,678)

4 Or that for which I live; who once again

5 I tender to thy hand: all thy vexations

Tender: "hand over" (Kittredge, 66); **vexations**: "torments" (Bevington, 61)

6 Were but my trials of thy love and thou

161

7 Hast strangely stood the test here, afore Heaven,

Strangely: "wonderfully well" (Riverside, 1,678)

8 I ratify this my rich gift. O Ferdinand,

9 Do not smile at me that I boast her off,

Boast her off: "i.e. praise her so highly" (Riverside, 1,678)

10 For thou shalt find she will outstrip all praise

11 And make it halt behind her.

Halt: "limp" (Riverside, 1,678)

FERDINAND

12 I do believe it

13 Against an oracle.

Against an oracle: "even if an oracle should declare otherwise" (Riverside, 1,679)

PROSPERO

14 Then, as my gift and thine own acquisition

15 Worthily purchased take my daughter: but

Purchased: "won" (Orgel, 171)

16 If thou dost break her virgin-knot before

17 All sanctimonious ceremonies may

Sanctimonious: "sacred, holy" (Riverside, 1,678)

18 With full and holy rite be minister'd,

19 No sweet aspersion shall the heavens let fall

Aspersion: "i.e. blessing; literally, sprinkling, as of rain that promotes fertility and growth" (Riverside, 1,678); "religious blessing" (Kittredge, 66)

20 To make this contract grow: but barren hate,

Grow: "be fruitful (as contrasted with *barren*)" (Riverside, 1,678); "develop into a happy marriage" (Kittredge, 66)

21 Sour-eyed disdain and discord shall bestrew

22 The union of your bed with weeds so loathly

Weeds: "instead of the flowers with which the marriage bed was customarily strewn" (Riverside, 1,678)

23 That you shall hate it both: therefore take heed,

24 As Hymen's lamps shall light you.

As . . . you: "i.e. as you desire happiness in your marriage. The symbolic torch of Hymen, god of marriage, was supposed to promise happiness if it burned with a clear flame, the opposite if it smoked." (Riverside, 1,678)

FERDINAND

25 As I hope

26 For quiet days, fair issue and long life,

Fair issue: "beautiful children" (Kittredge, 67)

27 With such love as 'tis now, the murkiest den,

Den: "originally the lair of a wild beast, and by extension any enclosed hiding place, generally with dangerous or unsavory overtones" (Orgel, 171)

28 The most opportune place, the strong'st suggestion.

Suggestion: "temptation" (Riverside, 1,679)

29 Our worser genius can, shall never melt   **Our . . . can**: "our bad angel is capable of" (Riverside, 1,679)

30 Mine honor into lust, to take away   **To**: "so as to" (Orgel, 172)

31 The edge of that day's celebration   **Edge**: "ardor, with explicit sexual connotations"; **that day's celebration / When**: "when the celebration of that day on which" (Orgel, 172)

32 When I shall think or Phoebus' steeds are founder'd,   **Or . . . founder'd**: "either the sun-god's horses have gone lame (because the day is so long)" (Riverside, 1,679); "i.e., that either day will never end or night will never come" (Langbaum, 98)

33 Or Night kept chain'd below.   **Below**: "Night was supposed to rise above the horizon as the sun sank below it" (Kittredge, 67)

PROSPERO

34 Fairly spoke.

35 Sit then and talk with her; she is thine own.

36 What, Ariel! my industrious servant, Ariel!   **What**: "now then" (Orgel, 172); "(summoning Ariel)" (Langbaum, 98)

Enter ARIEL

ARIEL

37 What would my potent master? here I am.

PROSPERO

38 Thou and thy meaner fellows your last service

Meaner fellows: "the 'meaner ministers' of 3.3.101" (Orgel, 172)

39 Did worthily perform; and I must use you

40 In such another trick. Go bring the rabble,

Trick: "ingenious device (technical term in Pageantry)"; **rabble**: "troop of inferior spirits" (Riverside, 1,679); "thy meaner fellows" (Langbaum, 98)

41 O'er whom I give thee power, here to this place:

42 Incite them to quick motion; for I must

43 Bestow upon the eyes of this young couple

44 Some vanity of mine art: it is my promise,

Vanity: "(1) illusion (2) trifle (3) desire for admiration, conceit" (Bevington, 62)

45 And they expect it from me.

ARIEL

46 Presently?

Presently: "immediately" (Riverside, 1,679)

PROSPERO

47 Ay, with a twink.

With a twink: "in a twinkling" (Riverside, 1,679)

Donald J. Richardson

ARIEL

48 Before you can say "come" and "go,"

49 And breathe twice and cry "so, so,"

50 Each one, tripping on his toe,

51 Will be here with mop and mow.

Mop and mow: "gesture and grimace" (Riverside, 1,679)

52 Do you love me, master? no?

PROSPERO

53 Dearly my delicate Ariel. Do not approach

54 Till thou dost hear me call.

ARIEL

55 Well, I conceive.

Conceive: "understand" (Riverside, 1,679)

Exit

PROSPERO

56 Look thou be true; do not give dalliance

True: "faithful to your word: Prospero returns to the question of Ferdinand's chastity"; **dalliance**: "originally simple conversation; by Chaucer's time the primary sense was 'flirtation, amorous toying'." (Orgel, 173)

57 Too much the rein: the strongest oaths are straw

58 To the fire i' the blood: be more abstenious,

Abstenious: "abstemious" (Riverside, 1,679)

59 Or else, good night your vow!

Good night: "i.e., say good-bye to" (Bevington, 63)

FERDINAND

60 I warrant you sir;

Warrant: "guarantee" (Bevington, 63)

61 The white cold virgin snow upon my heart

The . . . heart: "either the thought of Miranda enshrined in his heart, or his own chaste love for her." (Orgel, 173); "her pure white breast on mine (?)" (Langbaum, 99)

62 Abates the ardor of my liver.

Ardor: "heat" (Kittredge, 68); **liver**: "supposed seat of the passions" (Riverside, 1,679)

PROSPERO

63 Well.

64 Now come, my Ariel! bring a corollary,

Corollary: "surplus (of spirits)" (Langbaum, 99)

65 Rather than want a spirit: appear and pertly!

Want: "lack"; **pertly**: "briskly" (Riverside, 1,679)

66 No tongue! all eyes! be silent.

No tongue: "any speech from the spectators would make the spirits vanish. Cf. ll. 139-40." (Riverside, 1,679)

Donald J. Richardson

Soft music

Enter IRIS

Iris: "goddess of the rainbow and Juno's messenger" (Riverside, 1,679)

IRIS

67 Ceres, most bounteous lady, thy rich leas

Ceres: "goddess of agriculture"; **leas**: "meadows, cultivated land" (Riverside, 1,679)

68 Of wheat, rye, barley, fetches, oats and pease;

Fetches: "vetch, a fodder plant" (Riverside, 1,679)

69 Thy turfy mountains, where live nibbling sheep,

70 And flat meads thatch'd with stover, them to keep;

Meads . . . stover: "(meadows covered with a kind of grass used for winter fodder)" (Langbaum, 100)

71 Thy banks with pioned and twilled brims,

Pioned and twilled: "undercut by the stream and retained by interwoven branches" (Riverside, 1,679)

72 Which spungy April at thy hest betrims,

Spungy: "spongy, i.e. wet" (Riverside, 1,679); **hest**: "command"; **betrims**: "bedecks" (Kittredge, 69)

73 To make cold nymphs chaste crowns; and thy broom-groves,

Cold: "chaste"; **broom**: "a kind of shrub bearing yellow flowers" (Riverside, 1,679); **broom-groves**: "clumps of broom, gorse, yellow-flowered shrub" (Bevington, 63)

74 Whose shadow the dismissed bachelor loves,

Dismissed bachelor: "rejected suitor" (Riverside, 1,679)

75 Being lass-lorn: thy pole-clipt vineyard;

Lass-lorn: "forsaken by his sweetheart" (Kittredge, 69); **pole-clipt**: "poll-clipped, i.e. with top growth pruned back (?). If *clipt* means (as often) 'embraced,' the sense could be 'enclosed by a fence of poles' or 'with poles entwined by the vines.'" (Riverside, 1,679)

76 And thy sea-marge, sterile and rocky-hard,

Sea-marge: "seashore" (Kittredge, 69)

77 Where thou thyself dost air--the queen o' the sky,

Air: "take the air" (Langbaum, 100); **queen . . . sky**: "Juno" (Riverside, 1,679)

78 Whose watery arch and messenger am I,

Watery arch: "Iris as the rainbow" (Orgel, 175)

79 Bids thee leave these, and with her sovereign grace,

These: "'thy rich leas' and the other places just described" (Orgel, 175)

80 Here on this grass-plot, in this very place,

81 To come and sport: her peacocks fly amain:

Peacocks: "Juno's sacred birds, which drew her chariot"; **amain**: "swiftly" (Riverside, 1,679)

82 Approach, rich Ceres, her to entertain.

Entertain: "receive" (Riverside, 1,679)

Enter CERES

CERES

83 Hail, many-color'd messenger, that ne'er

84 Dost disobey the wife of Jupiter;

85 Who with thy saffron wings upon my flowers

Saffron: "yellow" (Kittredge, 69)

86 Diffusest honey-drops, refreshing showers,

87 And with each end of thy blue bow dost crown

Bow: "i.e., rainbow" (Bevington, 64)

88 My bosky acres and my unshrubb'd down,

Bosky: "wooded" (Riverside, 1,679); **unshrubb'd down**: "bare plains" (Orgel, 175); **down**: "upland" (Bevington, 64)

89 Rich scarf to my proud earth; why hath thy queen

90 Summon'd me hither, to this short-grass'd green?

Short-grass'd green: "There may be a specific reference here to the green rushes that covered the floor of the stage in public theaters . . . or to the green cloth that carpeted the dancing area when the Banqueting House was set up for a masque." (Orgel, 175)

IRIS

91 A contract of true love to celebrate;

92 And some donation freely to estate

Donation: "gift, blessing" (Kittredge, 70); **estate:** "bestow" (Riverside, 1,679)

93 On the blest lovers.

CERES

94 Tell me, heavenly bow,

Bow: "rainbow" (Orgel, 176)

95 If Venus or her son, as thou dost know,

Son: "Cupid, the 'blind boy' of line 98" (Riverside, 1,679); **as:** "so far as" (Orgel, 176)

96 Do now attend the queen? Since they did plot

97 The means that dusky Dis my daughter got,

Dusky: "both dark and melancholy." (Orgel, 176); **Dis**: "Pluto, ruler of the underworld (hence *dusky*), who carried off Ceres' daughter Proserpine to be his queen" (Riverside, 1,679); "The name means 'wealth': Pluto as god of the underworld was also god of riches. Dis is the Latin translation of the Green name, a shortened form of *Dives*, wealth." (Orgel, 176)

98 Her and her blind boy's scandall'd company

Her: "i.e., Venus" (Bevington, 64); **blind**: "Cupid was traditionally represented as blindfolded (hence 'love is blind')." (Orgel, 176); **scandall'd**: "scandalous" (Riverside, 1,679)

99 I have forsworn.

IRIS

100 Of her society

Society: "company" (Bevington, 64)

101 Be not afraid: I met her deity

Her deity: "jocular usage, on the model of 'his worship', 'her majesty', etc." (Orgel, 176)

102 Cutting the clouds towards Paphos and her son

Paphos: "place in Cyprus sacred to Venus" (Riverside, 1,679)

103 Dove-drawn with her. Here thought they to have done

Dove-drawn: "Venus' chariot was drawn by her sacred doves."; **done ... charm**: "cast some unchaste spell" (Riverside, 1,679)

104 Some wanton charm upon this man and maid,

To charm: "to inspire them with lust, as they did to Dis" (Orgel, 176)

105 Whose vows are, that no bed-right shall be paid

Bed-right shall be paid: "The bed-right involves the payment of a debt of homage to Hymen." (Orgel, 176)

106 Till Hymen's torch be lighted: but vain;

Till ... lighted: "till the marriage ceremony is performed" (Orgel, 176)

107 Mars's hot minion is return'd again;

Hot minion: "lustful mistress. Venus and Mars were lovers." **return'd**: "i.e. to Paphos" (Riverside, 1,679)

108 Her waspish-headed son has broke his arrows,

Waspish-headed: "irascible; and his arrows sting" (Orgel, 176)

109 Swears he will shoot no more but play with sparrows

Sparrows: "like doves, sacred to Venus. Sparrows were proverbially lecherous." (Riverside, 1,679)

110 And be a boy right out.

Be . . . out: "simply be a boy, give up his status as the god of love" (Orgel, 177); **right out**: "outright" (Kittredge, 70)

CERES

111 Highest queen of state,

Highest . . . state: "most majestic queen" (Riverside, 1,679)

112 Great Juno, comes; I know her by her gait.

Gait: "regal bearing" (Riverside, 1,680)

Enter JUNO

JUNO

113 How does my bounteous sister? Go with me

Bounteous sister: "i.e. because Ceres is goddess of the harvest" (Kittredge, 70); **go with me**: "This is more likely to be an invitation into the chariot than a proposal to promenade about the stage." (Orgel, 177)

114 To bless this twain, that they may prosperous be

115 And honor'd in their issue.

Issue: "offspring" (Bevington, 65)

They sing:

JUNO

116 Honor, riches, marriage-blessing,

117 Long continuance, and increasing,

118 Hourly joys be still upon you!

Still: "always"
(Riverside, 1,680)

119 Juno sings her blessings upon you.

CERES

120 Earth's increase, foison plenty,

Foison plenty: "plentiful
abundance"
(Riverside, 1,680)

121 Barns and garners never empty,

Garners: "granaries"
(Orgel, 177)

122 Vines and clustering bunches growing,

123 Plants with goodly burthen bowing;

124 Spring come to you at the farthest

Spring ... harvest: "i.e.,
may there be no winter in
your lives"
(Langbaum, 102)

125 In the very end of harvest!

In ... harvest: "i.e.
without intervening
winter" (Riverside, 1,680)

126 Scarcity and want shall shun you;

127 Ceres' blessing so is on you.

FERDINAND

128 This is a most majestic vision, and

129 Harmoniously charmingly. May I be bold

Charmingly:
"enchantingly, magically"
(Riverside, 1,680); **May
I be bold**: "Would I be
correct: for the boldness
involved, compare the
expression 'to venture an
opinion'." (Orgel, 178)

Donald J. Richardson

130 To think these spirits?

PROSPERO

131 Spirits, which by mine art

132 I have from their confines call'd to enact

Their confines: "the natural elements which they inhabit" (Orgel, 178)

133 My present fancies.

Fancies: "the same word as 'fantasies', and originally simply a shortened spelling." (Orgel, 178); "imaginative devices" (Kittredge, 71)

FERDINAND

134 Let me live here ever;

135 So rare a wonder'd father and a wise

So rare ... wise: "a father endowed with such rare and wonderful powers and such wisdom" (Kittredge, 71); **wonder'd**: "(1) to be wondered at; (2) able to perform wonders; (3) possessed of that wonder, Miranda" (Riverside, 1,680)

136 Makes this place Paradise.

Juno and Ceres whisper, and send Iris on employment

PROSPERO

137 Sweet now, silence!

Sweet now, silence: "addressed to Miranda, who is about to speak" (Riverside, 1,680)

138 Juno and Ceres whisper seriously;

139 There's something else to do: hush, and be mute,

140 Or else our spell is marr'd.

IRIS

141 You nymphs, call'd Naiads, of the windring brooks,

Nymphs: "The nymphs were the spirits of wild nature, pictured as beautiful young women. (The very word means 'young woman.')" (Asimov, 667); **Naiads**: "nymphs of springs, rivers, or lakes" (Bevington, 66); **windring**: "winding and wandering (apparently a coinage of Shakespeare's)" (Riverside, 1,680)

142 With your sedged crowns and ever-harmless looks,

Sedged: "made of reeds" (Bevington, 66); **sedged crowns**: "garlands of sedge, a river plant" (Orgel, 179); **ever-harmless**: "ever-innocent" (Riverside, 1,680)

143 Leave your crisp channels and on this green land

Crisp: "rippling" (Riverside, 1,680); **land**: "lawn" (Kittredge, 72)

144 Answer your summons; Juno does command:

145 Come, temperate nymphs, and help to celebrate

Temperate: "continent, chaste" (Kittredge, 72)

146 A contract of true love; be not too late.

Enter certain Nymphs

147 You sunburnt sicklemen, of August weary,

Sicklemen: "reapers"
(Kittredge, 72); **weary**:
"i.e., weary of the hard
work of the harvest"
(Bevington, 66)

148 Come hither from the furrow and be merry:

Furrow: "i.e., plowed
field" (Bevington, 66)

149 Make holiday; your rye-straw hats put on

150 And these fresh nymphs encounter every one

Fresh: "young and
beautiful"; **encounter**:
"meet" (Riverside, 1,680);
"join in dance"
(Kittredge, 72)

151 In country footing.

Country footing: "rustic
dancing" (Orgel, 179)

*Enter certain Reapers, properly habited: they join with the Nymphs in a
graceful dance; towards the end whereof PROSPERO starts suddenly, and
speaks; after which, to a strange, hollow, and confused noise, they heavily
vanish*

Properly: "appropriately"
(Orgel, 179*);**speaks*:
"(breaking the spell, which
depends on silence)"
(Langbaum, 103); **heavily**:
"reluctantly" (Riverside,
1,680); "slowly, dejectedly"
(Bevington, 66)

PROSPERO

152 [Aside] I had forgot that foul conspiracy

153 Of the beast Caliban and his confederates

154 Against my life: the minute of their plot

155 Is almost come.

To the Spirits

156 Well done! avoid; no more!

Avoid: "be gone"
(Riverside, 1,680)

FERDINAND

157 This is strange: your father's in some passion

158 That works him strongly.

Works: "agitates"
(Riverside, 1,680)

MIRANDA

159 Never till this day

160 Saw I him touch'd with anger so distemper'd.

Distemper'd: "literally, having the temper, or proportion, of the bodily humors disturbed. The term implies a physiological basis for vexation." (Orgel, 180)

PROSPERO

161 You do look, my son, in a mov'd sort,

Mov'd sort: "troubled state" (Riverside, 1,680)

162 As if you were dismay'd: be cheerful, sir.

163 Our revels now are ended. These our actors,

Revels: "festivity, entertainment" (Riverside, 1,680)

164 As I foretold you, were all spirits and

Foretold you: "previously told you (not 'predicted to you')" (Orgel, 180)

165 Are melted into air, into thin air:

166 And, like the baseless fabric of this vision,

Baseless fabric:
"structure without
physical foundation"
(Riverside, 1,680)

167 The cloud-capp'd towers, the gorgeous palaces,

168 The solemn temples, the great globe itself,

Great globe: "(with
a glance at the Globe
Theatre)" (Bevington, 67)

169 Ye all which it inherit, shall dissolve

Which it inherit: "who
occupy it"
(Riverside, 1,680)

170 And, like this insubstantial pageant faded,

Insubstantial: "without
material substance"
(Riverside, 1,680);
pageant: "another
technical term, like
'revels'. The basic
meanings are 'scene
acted upon the state',
'stage on which scenes
are performed', 'stage
machine', 'tableau or
allegorical device'; when
extended into the moral
sphere the word implied
deception, trickery,
specious or empty show."
(Orgel, 181)

171 Leave not a rack behind. We are such stuff

Rack: "wisp of cloud"
(Riverside, 1,680)

172 As dreams are made on, and our little life

On: "of" (Riverside, 1,680)

173 Is rounded with a sleep. Sir, I am vex'd;

Rounded with: "rounded
off by; brought to an end
by" (Kittredge, 73)

174 Bear with my weakness; my old brain is troubled:

175 Be not disturb'd with my infirmity: **With**: "by" (Orgel, 181)

176 If you be pleased, retire into my cell   **Retire**: "withdraw, go" (Bevington, 67)

177 And there repose: a turn or two I'll walk,

178 To still my beating mind.   **Beating**: "throbbing, agitated" (Orgel, 181)

FERDINAND MIRANDA

179 We wish your peace.

Exeunt

PROSPERO

180 Come with a thought I thank thee, Ariel: come.   **With**: "at the summon of" (Riverside, 1,680)

Enter ARIEL

ARIEL

181 Thy thoughts I cleave to. What's thy pleasure?   **Thy . . . cleave**: "I am ever at hand when thou thinkest of me" (Kittredge, 73); **cleave**: "cling adhere" (Bevington, 68)

PROSPERO

182 Spirit,

183 We must prepare to meet with Caliban.

Donald J. Richardson

ARIEL

184 Ay, my commander: when I presented Ceres,   **Presented**: "represented, took the part of (?)" (Riverside, 1,680)

185 I thought to have told thee of it, but I fear'd

186 Lest I might anger thee.

PROSPERO

187 Say again, where didst thou leave these varlots?   **Varlots**: "varlets, ruffians" (Riverside, 1,680)

ARIEL

188 I told you, sir, they were red-hot with drinking;

189 So fun of valor that they smote the air

190 For breathing in their faces; beat the ground

191 For kissing of their feet; yet always bending   **Bending**: "directing their steps" (Kittredge, 74); **bending ... project**: "pursuing their purpose— the murder of Prospero" (Riverside, 1,680)

192 Towards their project. Then I beat my tabor;   **Tabor**: "Ariel's side-drum" (Orgel, 182)

193 At which, like unback'd colts, they prick'd   **Unback'd**: "never ridden, unbroken" (Riverside, 1,680)

194 their ears,

195 Advanc'd their eyelids, lifted up their noses   **Advanc'd**: "raised" (Riverside, 1,680)

196 As they smelt music: so I charm'd their ears   **As**: "as if"
(Riverside, 1,680)

197 That calf-like they my lowing follow'd through   **Lowing**: "mooing"
(Bevington, 68)

198 Tooth'd briers, sharp furzes, pricking goss and thorns,   **Furzes, goss**: "forms
of the same plant"
(Orgel, 182); "gorse"
(Langbaum, 105);
"prickly shrubs"
(Bevington, 68)

199 Which entered their frail shins: at last I left them

200 I' the filthy-mantled pool beyond your cell,   **Filthy-mantled**:
"covered with dirty
scum"
(Riverside, 1,681)

201 There dancing up to the chins, that the foul lake   **That**: "so that"
(Orgel, 183)

202 O'erstunk their feet.   **O'erstunk**: "smelled
worse than, or, caused
to stink terribly"
(Bevington, 68)

PROSPERO

203 This was well done, my bird.   **Bird**: "youngster"
(Orgel, 183)

204 Thy shape invisible retain thou still:

205 The trumpery in my house, go bring it hither,   **Trumpery**: "showy
finery (the 'glistering
apparel' of line 213
s.d.)" (Riverside,
1,681); "rubbish"
(Kittredge, 74)

206 For stale to catch these thieves.

Stale: "bait, literally a stuffed bird or decoy used in hunting" (Kittredge, 74); "(1) decoy (2) out-of-fashion garments (with possibly further suggestions of *fit for a stale*, or prostitute, *stale* meaning 'horse piss,' l. 220, and *steal*, pronounced like *stale*)" (Bevington, 68)

ARIEL

207 I go, I go.

Exit

PROSPERO

208 A devil, a born devil, on whose nature

209 Nurture can never stick; on whom my pains,

Nurture: "training and education" (Kittredge, 74)

210 Humanely taken, all, all lost, quite lost;

211 And as with age his body uglier grows,

212 So his mind cankers. I will plague them all,

Cankers: "becomes malignant" (Riverside, 1,681)

213 Even to roaring.

Re-enter ARIEL, loaden with glistering apparel, & c

214 Come, hang them on this line.

Line: "lime tree, linden" (Riverside, 1,681)

PROSPERO and ARIEL remain invisible. Enter CALIBAN, STEPHANO, and TRINCULO, all wet

CALIBAN

215 Pray you, tread softly, that the blind mole may not   **Mole**: "thought to have sensitive hearing" (Riverside, 1,681)

216 Hear a foot fall: we now are near his cell.

STEPHANO

217 Monster, your fairy, which you say is

218 a harmless fairy, has done little better than

219 played the Jack with us.   **Jack**: "(1) knave; (2) jack-o'-lantern, i.e. will-o'-the-wisp" (Riverside, 1,681)

TRINCULO

220 Monster, I do smell all horse-piss; at

221 which my nose is in great indignation.

STEPHANO

222 So is mine. Do you hear, monster? If I should take

223 a displeasure against you, look you--

TRINCULO

224 Thou wert but a lost monster.

CALIBAN

225 Good my lord, give me thy favor still.

226 Be patient, for the prize I'll bring thee to   **Prize**: "booty" (Orgel, 184)

227 Shall hoodwink this mischance: therefore speak softly.

Hoodwink: "make you blind to" (Riverside, 1,681); "put out of sight" (Langbaum, 106); "cover up, make you not see (a hawking term)"; **mischance**: "mishap, misfortune" (Bevington, 69)

228 All's hush'd as midnight yet.

TRINCULO

229 Ay, but to lose our bottles in the pool--

STEPHANO

230 There is not only disgrace and dishonor in that,

231 monster, but an infinite loss.

TRINCULO

232 That's more to me than my wetting: yet this is your

233 harmless fairy, monster.

STEPHANO

234 I will fetch off my bottle, though I be o'er ears

Fetch off: "either rescue or drink up"; **o'er ears**: "i.e. drowned" (Orgel, 184)

235 for my labor.

CALIBAN

236 Prithee, my king, be quiet. Seest thou here,

237 This is the mouth o' the cell: no noise, and enter.

238 Do that good mischief which may make this island

239 Thine own for ever, and I, thy Caliban,

240 For aye thy foot-licker.

STEPHANO

241 Give me thy hand. I do begin to have bloody thoughts.

TRINCULO

242 O king Stephano! O peer! O worthy Stephano! Look

Peer: "referring to the old ballad 'King Stephen was a worthy peer,' quoted in *Othello*, II.iii.89-96" (Riverside, 1,681)

243 what a wardrobe here is for thee!

CALIBAN

244 Let it alone, thou fool; it is but trash.

TRINCULO

245 O, ho, monster! we know what belongs to a frippery.

Frippery: "secondhand-clothes shop" (Riverside, 1,681); "i.e., this is *not* trash" (Orgel, 185)

246 O king Stephano!

STEPHANO

247 Put off that gown, Trinculo; by this hand, I'll have

Put off: "take off" (Orgel, 185)

248 that gown.

TRINCULO

249 Thy grace shall have it.

CALIBAN

250 The dropsy drown this fool! what do you mean

Dropsy: "The disease is characterized by an excessive accumulation of fluid in the bodily tissues, and hence was used figuratively for an insatiable thirst or craving (OED 2)" (Orgel, 185); **drown**: "suffocate" (Riverside, 1,681)

251 To dote thus on such luggage? Let's alone

Luggage: "encumbering trash" (Riverside, 1,681); "literally, what must be lugged about" (Orgel, 185)

252 And do the murder first: if he awake,

253 From toe to crown he'll fill our skins with pinches,

Crown: "head" (Bevington, 70)

254 Make us strange stuff.

Stuff: "referring both to the 'luggage' of l. 251 and the fabric of the 'glistering apparel'. The line should be read emphasizing '*us*'." (Orgel, 185)

STEPHANO

255 Be you quiet, monster. Mistress line,

Mistress line: "(addressed to the linden or Lime Tree)" (Bevington, 70)

256 is not this my jerkin? Now is the jerkin under

Jerkin: "jacket made of leather" (Bevington, 70)"; **under the line**: "with pun on the sense 'south of the equator.' The joke involves the popular idea that travelers to tropical countries lost their hair through fevers, or from scurvy resulting from lack of fresh food on the long voyage." (Riverside, 1,681)

257 the line: now, jerkin, you are like to lose your

Line: "lime tree" (Kittredge, 76); "Stephano also quibbles bawdily on losing hair through syphilis, and in *Mistress* and *jerkin*"; **like**: "likely" (Bevington, 70)

258 hair and prove a bald jerkin.

Bald: "(1) hairless, napless (2) meager" (Bevington, 70); **jerkin**: "jacket" (Kittredge, 76)

TRINCULO

259 Do, do: we steal by line and level, and't like your grace.

Do, do: "an expression of approval, equivalent to 'bravo.'"; **by level**: "with plumb-line and carpenter's level, i.e. with professional skill (continuing the puns on *line*)"; **and't like**: "if it please" (Riverside, 1,681)

STEPHANO

260 I thank thee for that jest; here's a garment for't:

261 wit shall not go unrewarded while I am king of this

262 country. "Steal by line and level" is an excellent

263 pass of pate; there's another garment for't.

> **Pass**: "thrust (a fencing term); **pate**: "i.e. wit" (Riverside, 1,681)

TRINCULO

264 Monster, come, put some lime upon your fingers, and

> **Lime**: "sticky substance; thieves were jokingly said to have lime on their fingers" (Riverside, 1,681)

265 away with the rest.

CALIBAN

266 I will have none on't: we shall lose our time,

267 And all be turn'd to barnacles, or to apes

> **Barnacles**: "a kind of geese traditionally supposed to develop from the shellfish so named" (Riverside, 1,681); "here evidently used, like *apes*, as types of simpletons" (Bevington, 71)

268 With foreheads villainous low.

> **Villainous**: "wretchedly" (Riverside, 1,681)

STEPHANO

269 Monster, lay-to your fingers: help to bear this

> **Lay-to**: "apply"; **this**: "the clothing from the lime-tree" (Orgel, 186)

270 away where my hogshead of wine is, or I'll turn you **Hogshead**: "large cask" (Bevington, 71)

271 out of my kingdom: go to, carry this. **Go to**: "expression of exhortation or reproof, equivalent to 'come, come!'" (Riverside, 1,681)

TRINCULO

272 And this.

STEPHANO

273 Ay, and this.

A noise of hunters heard. Enter divers Spirits, in shape of dogs and hounds, and hunt them about, PROSPERO and ARIEL setting them on

PROSPERO

274 Hey, Mountain, hey! **Mountain ... Silver ... Fury ... Tyrant**: "names of hounds" (Kittredge, 77)

ARIEL

275 Silver I there it goes, Silver!

PROSPERO

276 Fury, Fury! there, Tyrant, there! hark! hark! **Hark**: "'sic 'em!'" (Riverside, 1,681)

CALIBAN, STEPHANO, and TRINCULO, are driven out

277 Go charge my goblins that they grind their joints

278 With dry convulsions, shorten up their sinews

Dry convulsions: "such as come when the joints are dry from old age and bone seems to grind upon bone" (Kittredge, 77); **convulsions**: "cramps" (Bevington, 72)

279 With aged cramps, and more pinch-spotted make them

Aged: "such as old people have" (Riverside, 1,681); **pinch-spotted**: "marked by the pinches of fairies and goblins" (Kittredge, 77)

280 Than pard or cat o' mountain.

Pard: "leopard"; **cat o' mountain**: "catamount, wildcat" (Riverside, 1,681)

ARIEL

281 Hark, they roar!

PROSPERO

282 Let them be hunted soundly. At this hour

Soundly: "thoroughly" (Bevington, 72)

283 Lies at my mercy all mine enemies:

284 Shortly shall all my labors end, and thou

285 Shalt have the air at freedom: for a little

Little: "little while longer" (Bevington, 72)

286 Follow, and do me service.

Exeunt

ACT V

SCENE I. Before PROSPERO'S cell.

Enter PROSPERO in his magic robes, and ARIEL

PROSPERO

1 Now does my project gather to a head:

> **Project**: "design, scheme; and, taken with *gather to a head* and *crack* (l. 2), suggesting an alchemical metaphor."; **gather to a head** "approach a crisis; perhaps more specifically come to a boil, as liquid, continuing the projection metaphor" (Orgel, 187)

2 My charms crack not; my spirits obey; and time

3 Goes upright with his carriage. How's the day?

> **Goes . . . carriage**: "walks upright under what he is carrying (because his burden of coming events has been greatly lightened)" (Riverside, 1,682)

ARIEL

4 On the sixt hour; at which time, my lord,

> **On**: "approaching"; **sixt**: "sixth. On the time, see I.ii.328-29" (Riverside, 1,682)

5 You said our work should cease.

Donald J. Richardson

PROSPERO

6 I did say so,

7 When first I raised the tempest. Say, my spirit,

8 How fares the king and's followers?

ARIEL

9 Confined together

10 In the same fashion as you gave in charge,

11 Just as you left them; all prisoners, sir,

12 In the line-grove which weather-fends your cell;

> **Line-grove**: "lime or linden grove" (Orgel, 188); **weather-fends**: "serves as windbreak for" (Riverside, 1,682)

13 They cannot boudge till your release. The king,

> **Boudge**: "budge, stir"; **your release**: "i.e. their release by you" (Riverside, 1,682)

14 His brother and yours, abide all three distracted

> **Distracted**: "out of their wits" (Riverside, 1,682)

15 And the remainder mourning over them,

16 Brimful of sorrow and dismay; but chiefly

17 Him that you term'd, sir, "The good old lord Gonzalo;"

18 His tears run down his beard, like winter's drops

19 From eaves of reeds. Your charm so strongly works 'em

> **Eaves of reeds**: "thatched roofs" (Riverside, 1,682)

194

20 That if you now beheld them, your affections

Affections:
"inclinations, bent
of mind" (Riverside,
1,682); "feelings"
(Orgel, 188)

21 Would become tender.

PROSPERO

22 Dost thou think so, spirit?

ARIEL

23 Mine would, sir, were I human.

PROSPERO

24 And mine shall.

25 Hast thou, which art but air, a touch, a feeling

Touch: "synonymous
with *feeling*"
(Riverside, 1,682);
"delicate perception"
(Orgel, 188)

26 Of their afflictions, and shall not myself,

27 One of their kind, that relish all as sharply,

Relish: "experience";
all: "quite"
(Riverside, 1,682)

28 Passion as they, be kindlier moved than thou art?

Passion: "(verb)"
(Langbaum, 109);
kindlier: "(1) more
sympathetically; (2)
more naturally (as
'one of their kind')"
(Riverside, 1,682)

29 Though with their high wrongs I am struck to the quick,

Quick: "the tenderest
or most vital part"
(Orgel, 188)

30 Yet with my nobler reason, 'gainst my fury

31 Do I take part: the rarer action is

Take part: "side"; **rarer**: "finer, nobler" (Riverside, 1,682)

32 In virtue than in vengeance: they being penitent,

Virtue: "a much broader concept than the expected 'forgiveness'."; **they . . . penitent**: "These conditions are not met" (Orgel, 189)

33 The sole drift of my purpose doth extend

Sole drift: "whole direction or tendency" (Kittredge, 79)

34 Not a frown further. Go release them, Ariel:

Not a frown further: "no farther than I have already gone—not even to the extent of a single angry look" (Kittredge, 79)

35 My charms I'll break, their senses I'll restore,

36 And they shall be themselves.

ARIEL

37 I'll fetch them, sir.

Exit

PROSPERO

38 Ye elves of hills, brooks, standing lakes and groves,

Standing: "having no tide or outlet" (Kittredge, 79)

39 And ye that on the sands with printless foot

Printless: "leaving no footprint" (Kittredge, 80)

40 Do chase the ebbing Neptune and do fly him

Ebbing Neptune: "outgoing tide" (Kittredge, 80); **fly**: "flee" (Orgel, 189); "fly with him" (Langbaum 110)

41 When he comes back; you demi-puppets that

Demi-puppets: "quasi-puppets, i.e. creatures of small size" (Riverside, 1,682)

42 By moonshine do the green sour ringlets make,

Green sour ringlets: "so-called 'fairy rings' in grass, actually caused by mushrooms" (Riverside, 1,682)

43 Whereof the ewe not bites, and you whose pastime

44 Is to make midnight mushrumps, that rejoice

Mushrumps: "mushrooms, supposed because of their rapid growth to be made by elves during the night" (Riverside, 1,682); **that**: "you who" (Orgel, 189)

45 To hear the solemn curfew; by whose aid,

Curfew: "supposedly spirits could be abroad only between curfew (9 p.m.) and the first cockcrow; cf. I.ii.450)" (Riverside, 1,682)

46 Weak masters though ye be, I have bedimm'd

Weak: "i.e. as compared with the powerful demons summoned up by black magic" (Riverside, 1,682); **masters**: "ministers or instruments" (Orgel, 190); **masters**: "masters of supernatural power" (Langbaum, 110)

47 The noontide sun, call'd forth the mutinous winds,   **Mutinous**: "stormy" (Kittredge, 80)

48 And 'twixt the green sea and the azur'd vault   **Azur'd vault**: "blue sky" (Kittredge, 80)

49 Set roaring war: to the dread rattling thunder   **To . . . fire**: "I have discharged the dread rattling thunderbolt" (Bevington, 74)

50 Have I given fire and rifted Jove's stout oak   **Rifted**: "split" (Riverside, 1,682); **Jove's . . . oak**: "The tree was sacred to Jove because of its hardness and endurance" (Orgel, 190)

51 With his own bolt; the strong-based promontory   **Bolt**: "lightning bolt" (Bevington, 74)

52 Have I made shake and by the spurs pluck'd up   **Spurs**: "roots" (Riverside, 1,682)

53 The pine and cedar: graves at my command

54 Have waked their sleepers, oped, and let 'em forth

55 By my so potent art. But this rough magic   **Rough**: "i.e. capable of producing the violent effects just described (?)" (Riverside, 1,682)

56 I here abjure, and, when I have requir'd   **Requir'd**: "requested" (Riverside, 1,682)

57 Some heavenly music, which even now I do,

58 To work mine end upon their senses that   **Their senses that**: "the senses of those whom" (Riverside, 1,682)

59 This airy charm is for, I'll break my staff,

Airy charm: "i.e. the music" (Riverside, 1,682); **I'll break ... my book**: "This passage has often been fancifully interpreted as Shakespeare's own farewell to the stage."; **staff**: "magic wand" (Kittredge, 80)

60 Bury it certain fathoms in the earth,

61 And deeper than did ever plummet sound

62 I'll drown my book.

My book: "the manuscript volume containing the formulas for controlling spirits" (Kittredge, 80-1)

Solemn music

Re-enter ARIEL before: then ALONSO, with a frantic gesture, attended by GONZALO, SEBASTIAN and ANTONIO in like manner, attended by ADRIAN and FRANCISCO. They all enter the circle which PROSPERO had made, and there stand charm'd; which PROSPERO observing, speaks:

Frantic gesture: "insane demeanor" (Riverside, 1,682); **Prospero ... speaks**: "Prospero is invisible and inaudible to the assembled company until he reveals himself at l. 112." (Orgel, 191)

63 A solemn air and the best comforter

Air: "song" (Bevington, 75); **and**: "i.e. which is" (Riverside, 1,682)

64 To an unsettled fancy cure thy brains,

Unsettled fancy: "disturbed imagination, here with implications of delusion and insanity" (Orgel, 191); **thy brains**: "the first sentence is addressed to Alonso, the next to all six now within the circle." (Riverside, 1,682)

65 Now useless, boil'd within thy skull! There stand,

Boil'd: "i.e. made useless by passion" (Riverside, 1,682

66 For you are spell-stopp'd.

67 Holy Gonzalo, honorable man,

68 Mine eyes, even sociable to the show of thine,

Sociable; "sympathetic"; **show**: "appearance" (Riverside, 1,682)

69 Fall fellowly drops. The charm dissolves apace,

Fall fellowly drops: "shed tear in sympathy" (Kittredge, 81)

70 And as the morning steals upon the night,

71 Melting the darkness, so their rising senses

72 Begin to chase the ignorant fumes that mantle

Ignorant fumes: "fumes that make them uncomprehending" (Riverside, 1,682); **mantle**: "envelop" (Bevington, 75)

73 Their clearer reason. O good Gonzalo,

Clearer: "growing clearer" (Orgel, 191)

74 My true preserver, and a loyal sir

Sir: "gentleman" (Orgel, 191)

75 To him you follow'st! I will pay thy graces

Pay ... Home: "reward
your favors fully"
(Riverside, 1,682);
graces: "virtues and
favors" (Kittredge, 81)

76 Home both in word and deed. Most cruelly

Home: "thoroughly"
(Kittredge, 81)

77 Didst thou, Alonso, use me and my daughter:

78 Thy brother was a furtherer in the act.

Furtherer:
"accomplice"
(Bevington, 75)

79 Thou art pinch'd for't now, Sebastian. Flesh and blood,

Pinch'd: "tortured,
punished" (Orgel, 192)

80 You, brother mine, that entertain'd ambition,

Entertain'd: "received
with welcome"
(Kittredge, 81)

81 Expell'd remorse and nature; who, with Sebastian,

Remorse: "pity";
nature: "natural feeling"
(Riverside, 1,682)

82 Whose inward pinches therefore are most strong,

Therefore: "therefor, to
that end"
(Riverside, 1,682)

83 Would here have kill'd your king; I do forgive thee,

84 Unnatural though thou art. Their understanding

85 Begins to swell, and the approaching tide

Swell: "rise (as the
sea rises when the
tide begins to flow)"
(Kittredge, 81)

86 Will shortly fill the reasonable shores

Reasonable shores:
"shores of reason, i.e.
minds"
(Riverside, 1,683)

Donald J. Richardson

87 That now lies foul and muddy. Not one of them

Not one of them: "'There is' understood" (Orgel, 192)

88 That yet looks on me, or would know me! Ariel,

89 Fetch me the hat and rapier in my cell:

Hat and rapier: "These are essential elements of aristocratic dress" (Orgel, 192)

90 I will discase me, and myself present

Discase me: "take off my magician's robe" (Riverside, 1,683); "disrobe" (Langbaum, 111)

91 As I was sometime Milan: quickly, spirit;

As . . . Milan: "dressed as I formerly was as Duke of Milan" (Riverside, 1,683)

92 Thou shalt ere long be free.

ARIEL sings and helps to attire him

93 Where the bee sucks, there suck I:

Where . . . bough: "The song is Ariel's proleptic celebration of freedom." (Orgel, 193)

94 In a cowslip's bell I lie;

95 There I couch when owls do cry.

Couch: "lie" (Kittredge, 82)

96 On the bat's back I do fly

97 After summer merrily.

After summer: "pursuing summer, as birds migrate when the weather grows cold. Ariel anticipates a life of everlasting summer, as Prospero's masque had promised the lovers a world without winter." (Orgel, 193)

98 Merrily, merrily shall I live now

99 Under the blossom that hangs on the bough.

PROSPERO

100 Why, that's my dainty Ariel! I shall miss thee:

101 But yet thou shalt have freedom: so, so, so.

So, so, so: "probably an expression of approval as Ariel finishes attiring him" (Riverside, 1,683)

102 To the king's ship, invisible as thou art:

103 There shalt thou find the mariners asleep

104 Under the hatches; the master and the boatswain

105 Being awake, enforce them to this place,

Being awake: "after they have waked up" (Kittredge, 82)

106 And presently, I prithee.

Presently: "at once" (Riverside, 1,683)

ARIEL

107 I drink the air before me, and return

Drink the air: "consume space, devour the way" (Kittredge, 82-3)

108 Or ere your pulse twice beat.

Or ere: "Both words mean 'before'" (Orgel, 193)

Exit

GONZALO

109 All torment, trouble, wonder and amazement

110 Inhabits here: some heavenly power guide us

111 Out of this fearful country!

Fearful: "frightening" (77)

PROSPERO

112 Behold, sir king,

113 The wronged Duke of Milan, Prospero:

114 For more assurance that a living prince

For more assurance: "to make thee more sure" (Kittredge, 83); **a living prince**: "i.e. not a spirit" (Riverside, 1,683)

115 Does now speak to thee, I embrace thy body;

116 And to thee and thy company I bid

117 A hearty welcome.

ALONSO

118 Whe'er thou beest he or no,

Whe'er: "for 'whether'" (Orgel, 194)

119 Or some enchanted trifle to abuse me,

Enchanted trifle: "trick of magic"; **abuse**: "deceive" (Riverside, 1,683)

120 As late I have been, I not know: thy pulse

Late: "lately" (Bevington, 77); **have been**: "i.e. abused" (Orgel, 194)

121 Beats as of flesh and blood; and, since I saw thee,

122 The affliction of my mind amends, with which,

123 I fear, a madness held me: this must crave,

This . . . story: "this demands, if it is really taking place, an extraordinary explanation" (Riverside, 1,683); **crave**: "call for" (Orgel, 194); "require" (Bevington, 77)

124 An if this be at all, a most strange story.

An ... all: "if this is not another illusion" (Orgel, 194); **story**: "i.e., explanation" (Bevington, 77)

125 Thy dukedom I resign and do entreat

126 Thou pardon me my wrongs. But how should Prospero

My wrongs: "the wrongs I have done you" (Orgel, 194)

127 Be living and be here?

PROSPERO

128 First, noble friend,

129 Let me embrace thine age, whose honor cannot

Thine age: "i.e. thy reverend self"; **cannot ... confin'd**: "i.e. is immeasurable and boundless" (Riverside, 1,683)

130 Be measured or confin'd.

GONZALO

131 Whether this be

132 Or be not, I'll not swear.

PROSPERO

133 You do yet taste

Taste: "experience, feel" (Kittredge, 83)

134 Some subtleties o' the isle, that will not let you **Subleties**: "illusions, with
play (as *taste* suggests)
on the word as applied
to fancy confections
representing actual objects
or allegorical figures"
(Riverside, 1,683)

135 Believe things certain. Welcome, my friends all! **Things certain**: "things
indubitably real (and not
the products of magic)"
(Kittredge, 83)

Aside to SEBASTIAN and ANTONIO

136 But you, my brace of lords, were I so minded, **Brace**: "pair" (Orgel, 194)

137 I here could pluck his highness' frown upon you **Pluck**: "bring down"
(Kittredge, 83)

138 And justify you traitors: at this time **Justify**: "prove"
(Riverside, 1,683)

139 I will tell no tales. **No**: "most likely
a repetition of his
determination to 'tell no
tales'." (Orgel, 194)

SEBASTIAN

140 [Aside] The devil speaks in him.

PROSPERO

141 No.

142 For you, most wicked sir, whom to call brother

143 Would even infect my mouth, I do forgive

144 Thy rankest fault; all of them; and require **Require**: "request"
(Kittredge, 84)

145 My dukedom of thee, which perforce, I know,

Perforce: "necessarily" (Bevington, 78)

146 Thou must restore.

ALONSO

147 If thou be'st Prospero,

148 Give us particulars of thy preservation;

149 How thou hast met us here, who three hours since

Three hours since: "This shows the surprisingly short time covered by the incidents of the play. . . . Shakespeare has observed the unity of time as well as the unity of place."(Kittredge, 84)

150 Were wrack'd upon this shore; where I have lost--

Wrack'd: "shipwrecked" (Kittredge, 84)

151 How sharp the point of this remembrance is!--

Sharp: "The memory stabs him to the heart" (Kittredge, 84)

152 My dear son Ferdinand.

PROSPERO

153 I am woe for't, sir.

Woe: "sorry" (Orgel, 195)

ALONSO

154 Irreparable is the loss, and patience

Patience: "calm endurance, fortitude under affliction" (Kittredge, 84)

155 Says it is past her cure.

PROSPERO

156 I rather think

157 You have not sought her help, of whose soft grace

> **Of . . . grace**: "by whose mercy" (Riverside, 1,683)

158 For the like loss I have her sovereign aid

> **Sovereign**: "most powerful" (Kittredge, 84)

159 And rest myself content.

> **Rest myself content**: "remain happy myself" (Kittredge, 84)

ALONSO

160 You the like loss!

PROSPERO

161 As great to me as late; and, supportable

> **As great to me, as late**: "as great to me as your loss, and as recent" (Langbaum, 114); **supportable . . . have I**: "to make the deeply felt loss bearable, I have" (Bevington, 78)

162 To make the dear loss, have I means much weaker

> **Dear**: "deeply felt" (Riverside, 1,683)

163 Than you may call to comfort you, for I

> **Comfort**: "support, strengthen" (Kittredge, 84)

164 Have lost my daughter.

ALONSO

165 A daughter?

166 O heavens, that they were living both in Naples, **That:** "provided that (i.e. if my death would bring it about)" (Orgel, 195)

167 The king and queen there! that they were, I wish **That:** "provided that" (Riverside, 1,683)

168 Myself were mudded in that oozy bed **Mudded:** "buried in the mud" (Bevington, 78)

169 Where my son lies. When did you lose your daughter?

PROSPERO

170 In this last tempest. I perceive these lords

171 At this encounter do so much admire **Encounter:** "meeting" (Orgel, 196); **admire:** "marvel" (Riverside, 1,683)

172 That they devour their reason and scarce think **Devour their reason:** "presumably referring to the open-mouthed astonishment in which their rational powers are lost" (Riverside, 1,683); **scarce . . . breath:** "scarcely believe that their eyes inform them accurately what they see or that their words are naturally spoken" (Bevington, 79)

173 Their eyes do offices of truth, their words **Do . . . truth:** "function accurately" (Riverside, 1,683)

174 Are natural breath: but, howsoe'er you have **Natural breath:** "such speech as we might expect from ordinary human beings" (Kittredge, 85)

175 Been justled from your senses, know for certain

176 That I am Prospero and that very duke

177 Which was thrust forth of Milan, who most strangely **Of**: "from" (Riverside, 1,683); **strangely**: "wonderfully" (Orgel, 196)

178 Upon this shore, where you were wreck'd, was landed,

179 To be the lord on't. No more yet of this;

180 For 'tis a chronicle of day by day, **Of day by day**: "to be told over many days" (Orgel, 196)

181 Not a relation for a breakfast nor **Relation**: "story" (Orgel, 196)

182 Befitting this first meeting. Welcome, sir;

183 This cell's my court: here have I few attendants

184 And subjects none abroad: pray you, look in. **Abroad**: "i.e. elsewhere on the island" (Riverside, 1,683)

185 My dukedom since you have given me again,

186 I will requite you with as good a thing; **Requite**: "repay" (Bevington, 79)

187 At least bring forth a wonder, to content ye **Bring forth a wonder**: "Prospero, punning on Miranda's name, seems to promise another illusion" (Orgel, 196)

188 As much as me my dukedom.

*Here PROSPERO discovers FERDINAND
and MIRANDA playing at chess*

Discovers: "discloses (by
pulling aside a curtain)"
(Riverside, 1,684)

MIRANDA

189 Sweet lord, you play me false.

Play me false: "cheat"
(Kittredge, 85)

FERDINAND

190 No, my dear'st love,

191 I would not for the world.

MIRANDA

192 Yes, for a score of kingdoms you should wrangle,

Yes . . . wrangle: "i.e.
certainly you should do
so for the world; in fact,
for less than the world—
for twenty kingdoms you
ought to do your utmost
against me" (Riverside,
1,684)

193 And I would call it, fair play.

ALONSO

194 If this prove

195 A vision of the Island, one dear son

Vision: "i.e. illusion"
(Riverside, 1,684)

196 Shall I twice lose.

Donald J. Richardson

SEBASTIAN

197 A most high miracle!

> **A . . . miracle**: "Sebastian is either for once impressed, or merely being characteristically sarcastic." (Orgel, 197)

FERDINAND

198 Though the seas threaten, they are merciful;

199 I have cursed them without cause.

Kneels

ALONSO

200 Now all the blessings

201 Of a glad father compass thee about!

> **Compass**: "emcompass, embrace" (Bevington, 80)

202 Arise, and say how thou camest here.

MIRANDA

203 O, wonder!

204 How many goodly creatures are there here!

> **Goodly**: "handsome" (Kittredge, 86)

205 How beauteous mankind is! O brave new world,

> **Mankind**: "presumably humanity; but, other than Miranda, there are only men present." (Orgel, 198); **brave**: "splendid, gorgeously appareled, handsome" (Bevington, 80)

206 That has such people in't!

PROSPERO

207 'Tis new to thee.

> **'Tis new to thee**: "Spoken with the tender and sadly reminiscent indulgence of age for the illusions of youth and inexperience." (Kittredge, 86)

ALONSO

208 What is this maid with whom thou wast at play?

209 Your eld'st acquaintance cannot be three hours:

> **Eld'st**: "longest possible" (Riverside, 1,684)

210 Is she the goddess that hath sever'd us,

211 And brought us thus together?

FERDINAND

212 Sir, she is mortal;

213 But by immortal Providence she's mine:

214 I chose her when I could not ask my father

215 For his advice, nor thought I had one. She

216 Is daughter to this famous Duke of Milan,

217 Of whom so often I have heard renown,

218 But never saw before; of whom I have

219 Received a second life; and second father

220 This lady makes him to me.

ALONSO

221 I am hers:

> **I am hers**: "I am her servant; my respects to her" (Orgel, 198); "I am her father; I accept her as my daughter." (Kittredge, 86)

222 But, O, how oddly will it sound that I

223 Must ask my child forgiveness!

PROSPERO

224 There, sir, stop:

225 Let us not burthen our remembrance with

226 A heaviness that's gone.

> **Heaviness**: "sadness, grief, bitter experience" (Kittredge, 86)

GONZALO

227 I have inly wept,

> **Inly**: "inwardly" (Bevington, 80)

228 Or should have spoke ere this. Look down, you god,

229 And on this couple drop a blessed crown!

230 For it is you that have chalk'd forth the way

> **Chalk'd forth the way**: "marked the true path as with a chalk line" (Orgel, 198)

231 Which brought us hither.

ALONSO

232 I say, Amen, Gonzalo!

GONZALO

233 Was Milan thrust from Milan, that his issue

Milan . . . Milan: "the Duke . . . the city" (Riverside, 1,684)

234 Should become kings of Naples? O, rejoice

235 Beyond a common joy, and set it down

236 With gold on lasting pillars: In one voyage

237 Did Claribel her husband find at Tunis,

238 And Ferdinand, her brother, found a wife

239 Where he himself was lost, Prospero his dukedom

240 In a poor isle and all of us ourselves

All . . . own: "we all found ourselves when every man was deluded" (Riverside, 1,684)

241 When no man was his own.

When . . . own: "when we had lost our senses" (Orgel, 199)

ALONSO

242 [To FERDINAND and MIRANDA] Give me your hands:

243 Let grief and sorrow still embrace his heart

Still: "ever"; **his heart / That**: "the heart of anyone who" (Riverside, 1,684); **embrace**: "cling to" (Kittredge, 87)

244 That doth not wish you joy!

GONZALO

245 Be it so! Amen!

Re-enter ARIEL, with the Master and Boatswain
amazedly following

Amazedly: "as in a
maze, in bewilderment"
(Riverside, 1,684)

246 O, look, sir, look, sir! here is more of us:

247 I prophesied, if a gallows were on land,

248 This fellow could not drown. Now, blasphemy,

Blasphemy: "blasphemous
fellow. Cf. *diligence* (=
diligent creature) in line
274." (Riverside, 1,684)

249 That swear'st grace o'erboard, not an oath on shore?

That . . . o'erboard:
"who are profane enough
to make heavenly
grace forsake the ship"
(Riverside, 1,684); **not
an oath**: "aren't you
going to swear an oath"
(Bevington, 81)

250 Hast thou no mouth by land? What is the news?

BOATSWAIN

251 The best news is, that we have safely found

Safely: "in a state of
safety" (Kittredge, 88)

252 Our king and company; the next, our ship--

253 Which, but three glasses since, we gave out split--

Glasses: "i.e. hours"; **gave
out**: "reported" (Riverside,
1,684)

254 Is tight and yare and bravely rigg'd as when

Yare: "shipshape"
(Riverside, 1,684);
Bravely: "splendidly"
(Bevington, 81)

255 We first put out to sea.

ARIEL

256 [Aside to PROSPERO] Sir, all this service

257 Have I done since I went.

PROSPERO

258 [Aside to ARIEL] My tricksy spirit!　　　　　　　**Tricksy**: "ingenious, adroit" (Riverside, 1,684)

ALONSO

259 These are not natural events; they strengthen　　**Strengthen ... stranger**: "increase in strangeness" (Riverside, 1,684)

260 From strange to stranger. Say, how came you hither?

BOATSWAIN

261 If I did think, sir, I were well awake,

262 I'ld strive to tell you. We were dead of sleep,　　**Of sleep**: "asleep" (Riverside, 1,684)

263 And--how we know not--all clapp'd under hatches;

264 Where but even now with strange and several noises　**Several**: "diverse" (Orgel, 200)

265 Of roaring, shrieking, howling, jingling chains,

266 And moe diversity of sounds, all horrible,　　　　**Moe**: "more" (Riverside, 1,684)

267 We were awaked; straightway, at liberty;　　　　**At liberty**: "i.e. no longer under hatches" (Riverside, 1,684)

268 Where we, in all our trim, freshly beheld

Our trim . . . ship: "i.e. our garments, like our ship, were undamaged" (Orgel, 200)

269 Our royal, good and gallant ship, our master

Our master: "the captain" (Kittredge, 88)

270 Cap'ring to eye her: on a trice, so please you,

Cap'ring to eye: "dancing to see" (Langbaum, 117); **on**: "in" (Riverside, 1,684)

271 Even in a dream, were we divided from them

Them: "the other members of the crew" (Orgel, 200)

272 And were brought moping hither.

Moping: "in a daze" (Riverside, 1,684)

ARIEL

273 [Aside to PROSPERO] Was't well done?

PROSPERO

274 [Aside to ARIEL] Bravely, my diligence. Thou shalt be free.

Bravely: "splendidly"; **diligence**: "diligent one" (Kittredge, 88)

ALONSO

275 This is as strange a maze as e'er men trod

276 And there is in this business more than nature

More . . . conduct of:
"more than nature ever
was director of; more than
what can be due to natural
causes" (Kittredge, 88)

277 Was ever conduct of: some oracle

Conduct: "conductor"
(Riverside, 1,684); **some
oracle . . . knowledge:**
"we need a revelation
from heaven to prove the
truth of what we seem to
know" (Kitrtredge, 88)

278 Must rectify our knowledge.

PROSPERO

279 Sir, my liege,

Liege: "sovereign"
(Riverside, 1,684)

280 Do not infest your mind with beating on

Infest: "annoy"
(Riverside, 1,684);
beating: "hammering,
insistently thinking"
(Orgel, 201)

281 The strangeness of this business; at pick'd leisure

Pick'd: "convenient"
(Riverside, 1,684)

282 Which shall be shortly, single I'll resolve you,

Single: "by myself
(without an oracle)"
(Riverside, 1,684);
resolve you: "clear up
your doubts; solve all
the problems for you"
(Kittredge, 89)

283 Which to you shall seem probable, of every

Probable: "satisfactory"
(Riverside, 1,685); **of every
These**: "about every one of
these" (Bevington, 82)

284 These happen'd accidents; till when, be cheerful

Accidents: "occurrences" (Riverside, 1,685)

285 And think of each thing well.

Well: "favorably" (Orgel, 201)

Aside to ARIEL

286 Come hither, spirit:

287 Set Caliban and his companions free;

288 Untie the spell.

Untie the spell: "Enchanted characters are regularly described in the play as 'knit up'." (Orgel, 201)

Exit ARIEL

289 How fares my gracious sir?

290 There are yet missing of your company

291 Some few odd lads that you remember not.

Odd: "unaccounted for" (Riverside, 1,685)

Re-enter ARIEL, driving in CALIBAN, STEPHANO and TRINCULO, in their stolen apparel

STEPHANO

292 Every man shift for all the rest, and

Every . . . rest: "Stephano drunkenly inverts the proverbial 'Every man for himself.'" (Riverside, 1,685)

293 let no man take care for himself; for all is

294 but fortune. Coraggio, bully-monster, coraggio!

Coraggio: "courage (Italian)" (Riverside, 1,685); **bully**: "'A term of endearment and familiarity. . . . Often prefixed as a sort of title to the name or designation of the person addressed' (OED 1)" (Orgel, 201)

TRINCULO

295 If these be true spies which I

If . . . head: "if my eyes can be trusted" (Orgel, 201); **true spies**: "reliable observers (eyes)" (Riverside, 1,685)

296 here's a goodly sight.

CALIBAN

297 O Setebos, these be brave spirits indeed!

Setebos: "the god of Caliban's mother" (Langbaum, 118); **brave**: "handsome, impressive" (Orgel, 202)

298 How fine my master is! I am afraid

Fine: "splendidly dressed (in his ducal robes)" (Riverside, 1,685)

299 He will chastise me.

SEBASTIAN

300 Ha, ha!

301 What things are these, my lord Antonio?

302 Will money buy 'em?

ANTONIO

303 Very like; one of them

304 Is a plain fish, and, no doubt, marketable.

Fish: "recalling Trinculo's doubt about whether Caliban was more like a man or a fish: see 2.2.30 ff." (Orgel, 202)

PROSPERO

305 Mark but the badges of these men, my lords,

Badges: "insignia for servants, indicating what master they served. Stephano and Trinculo are of course dressed in stolen garments." (Riverside, 1,685)

306 Then say if they be true. This mis-shapen knave,

True: "honest" (Riverside, 1,685)

307 His mother was a witch, and one so strong

308 That could control the moon, make flows and ebbs,

Make flows and ebbs: "as the moon does" (Orgel, 202)

309 And deal in her command without her power.

Her command: "i.e. the moon's authority"; **without her power**: "beyond the moon's influence" (Riverside, 1,685)

310 These three have robb'd me; and this demi-devil--

311 For he's a bastard one--had plotted with them

Bastard: "counterfeit" (Bevington, 83)

312 To take my life. Two of these fellows you

313 Must know and own; this thing of darkness! **Own**: "recognize, admit
                                                 as belonging to you"
                                                 (Bevington, 83)

314 Acknowledge mine.

CALIBAN

315 I shall be pinch'd to death.

ALONSO

316 Is not this Stephano, my drunken butler?

SEBASTIAN

317 He is drunk now: where had he wine?

ALONSO

318 And Trinculo is reeling ripe: where should they **Reeling ripe**: "ready (i.e.
                                                     drunk enough) for reeling"
                                                     (Orgel, 202)

319 Find this grand liquor that hath gilded 'em? **Gilded 'em**: "flushed
                                                  their faces (a common
                                                  connection between
                                                  blood and gold). Possibly
                                                  grand liquor contains
                                                  an alchemical allusion
                                                  to the long-sought elixir
                                                  that could transform
                                                  base substances to gold."
                                                  (Riverside, 1,685)

320 How camest thou in this pickle? **Pickle**: "both 'preserving
                                     liquor' and 'predicament'."
                                     (Orgel, 202)

Donald J. Richardson

TRINCULO

321 I have been in such a pickle since I

Pickle: "here alluding to his dousing in 'the foul lake'" (Orgel, 203)

322 saw you last that, I fear me, will never out of

323 my bones: I shall not fear fly-blowing.

Fly-blowing: "infestation by maggots (to which unpickled meat would be subject)" (Riverside, 1,685)

SEBASTIAN

324 Why, how now, Stephano!

STEPHANO

325 O, touch me not; I am not Stephano, but a cramp.

PROSPERO

326 You'ld be king o' the isle, sirrah?

Sirrah: "form of address to an inferior" (Riverside, 1,685)

STEPHANO

327 I should have been a sore one then.

Sore: "(1) harsh; (2) pain-wracked" (Riverside, 1,685)

ALONSO

328 This is a strange thing as e'er I look'd on.

Pointing to Caliban

PROSPERO

329 He is as disproportion'd in his manners

> **Manners**: "both 'forms of behavior' and 'moral character'" (Orgel, 203)

330 As in his shape. Go, sirrah, to my cell;

331 Take with you your companions; as you look

332 To have my pardon, trim it handsomely.

> **Trim**: "prepare, with implications of both 'make neat' and 'decorate'" (Orgel, 203)

CALIBAN

333 Ay, that I will; and I'll be wise hereafter

334 And seek for grace. What a thrice-double ass

> **Grace**: "forgiveness, favor" (Orgel, 203)

335 Was I, to take this drunkard for a god

336 And worship this dull fool!

PROSPERO

337 Go to; away!

ALONSO

338 Hence, and bestow your luggage where you found it.

> **Luggage**: "the stolen garments; the term is contemptuous, as in 4.1.269." (Orgel, 203)

SEBASTIAN

339 Or stole it, rather.

Exeunt CALIBAN, STEPHANO, and TRINCULO

PROSPERO

340 Sir, I invite your highness and your train

341 To my poor cell, where you shall take your rest

342 For this one night; which, part of it, I'll waste   **Waste**: "use up"
(Riverside, 1,685)

343 With such discourse as, I not doubt, shall make it

344 Go quick away; the story of my life

345 And the particular accidents gone by   **Accidents**: "events"
(Orgel, 204)

346 Since I came to this isle: and in the morn

347 I'll bring you to your ship and so to Naples,   **Bring**: "accompany"
(Orgel, 204)

348 Where I have hope to see the nuptial

349 Of these our dear-beloved solemnized;

350 And thence retire me to my Milan, where   **Retire me**: "return"
(Bevington, 85)

351 Every third thought shall be my grave.   **Every ... grave**: "This
may be more than the
conventional *memento
mori*" (Orgel, 204)

ALONSO

352 I long

353 To hear the story of your life, which must

354 Take the ear strangely.

Take: "enchant" (Riverside, 1,685); **strangely**: "wonderfully" (Orgel, 204)

PROSPERO

355 I'll deliver all;

Deliver: "report" (Riverside, 1,685)

356 And promise you calm seas, auspicious gales

357 And sail so expeditious that shall catch

Sail: "voyage" (Riverside, 1,685); **catch**: "catch up with" (Langbaum, 120)

358 Your royal fleet far off.

Far off: "the other ships are a day's journey ahead" (Orgel, 204)

Aside to ARIEL

359 My Ariel, chick,

Chick: "an affectionate epithet" (Orgel, 204)

360 That is thy charge: then to the elements

361 Be free, and fare thou well! Please you, draw near.

Draw near: "i.e. enter the cell" (Riverside, 1,685)

Exeunt

Epilogue

"There is no sound reason for suspecting that Shakespeare did not himself write the epilogue." (Kittredge, 92-3)

SPOKEN BY PROSPERO

1 Now my charms are all o'erthrown,

2 And what strength I have's mine own,

3 Which is most faint: now, 'tis true,

4 I must be here confin'd by you,
Confin'd: "held captive" (Kittredge, 93)

5 Or sent to Naples. Let me not,

6 Since I have my dukedom got

7 And pardon'd the deceiver, dwell

8 In this bare island by your spell;

9 But release me from my bands
Bands: "bonds" (Riverside, 1,685)

10 With the help of your good hands:
Hands: "i.e. applause. The noise of clapping would break the charm." (Riverside, 1,685)

229

11 Gentle breath of yours my sails

Gentle breath: "a favorable breeze (produced by hands clapping)" (Riverside, 1,685); "kind words (i.e. about the performance)" (Orgel, 205)

12 Must fill, or else my project fails,

13 Which was to please. Now I want

Want: "lack" (Riverside, 1,686)

14 Spirits to enforce, art to enchant,

Enforce: "control" (Orgel, 205)

15 And my ending is despair,

16 Unless I be relieved by prayer,

Prayer: "i.e. this petition" (Riverside, 1,686)

17 Which pierces so that it assaults

Assaults: "storms the ear of" (Riverside, 1,686)

18 Mercy itself and frees all faults.

Frees: "remits" (Riverside, 1,686)

19 As you from crimes would pardon'd be,

Crimes: "sins" (Riverside, 1,686)

20 Let your indulgence set me free.

Indulgence: "playing on the technical sense of remission of the punishment for sin" (Orgel, 205)

Works Cited

Asimov, Isaac. *Asimov's Guide to Shakespeare.* Vol. 1, The Greek, Roman, and Italian Plays, New York: Avanel Books, 1970, 650-670.

Bevington, David, Ed. *The Tempest.* New York: Bantam Books, 1988.

Kittredge, George Lyman, Ed. *The Tempest.* Waltham, Massachusetts: Blaisdell Publishing Company, 1966.

Landbaum, Robert, Ed. *The Tempest.* New York: Penguin Books, 1987.

Merrian-Webster's *Collegiate Dictionary,* Eleventh Edition. Springfield, Massachusetts: Merriam-Webster, Incorporated, 2003.

Orgel, Stephen, Ed. *The Tempest.* Oxford: Oxford University Press, 1987.

Shakespeare, William. *The Riverside Shakespeare.* 2nd Edition. Boston: Houghton Mifflin Company, 1997.

Lightning Source UK Ltd.
Milton Keynes UK
UKOW03f1042180814

237103UK00001B/252/P